Legends of the Longsword

Mercenary Series: Book Two

J.W. Webb

Acknowledgement for:
John Jarrold, for editing
Roger Garland, for the illustrations
Ravven, for cover design
Jason & Marina of Polgarus Studio, for book design and formatting.

For Terry Bates
News South Wales Beer Drinking Champion, and fellow Zebu Pirate

Check out the series here jwwebbauthor.com and join the VIP Lounge for more Free books. You'll find more details and a sample at the back of this book.

Contents

Part One
Outlaws

Chapter 1 | The Crimson Moon

"Got your attention?" The poniard quivered on the table top, and twenty pairs of eyes looked his way - including the proprietor, who'd been ignoring him these last ten minutes. "Good. Hate to think you were avoiding me." Hagan smiled, removed the dagger and thrust it back in his sheath.

"We are busy today," the innkeep looked worried. For good reason. Rough tavern, wrong side of town. And some local gang members already well into their cups.

Hagan glanced casually over to the corner table where four big swarthy individuals turned their heads away and continued with their dice game. "Not sensible, drawing attention to yourself, stranger," the innkeep said, his worried glance on the mark left by Hagan's dagger.

"I think you're worried enough for both of us," Hagan yawned snatched the ale from the proprietor's sweaty hands and downed three-quarters. "That's better." Thanks. Been a long week." He managed a rare smile.

The man nodded and turned to another customer, but Hagan grabbed his collar checking him. "Name?"

"Rezala," the innkeep mumbled. Hagan let go and the man dusted down his collar. He looked alarmed – stressed.

"And this place?"

"*The Crimson Moon*. Did you not see the sign above the door?"

"No," Hagan said draining his tankard and shoving it on the table. "Another. *Please*." He smiled again—rare that. *I must be in a good mood. Won't last—never does.*

"You can go now," Hagan winked at innkeep Rezala. "Customers waiting," he pointed to the far side of the room where three large men had just appeared. They looked as thirsty as Hagan had been. They also looked violent and angry—ready for trouble.

Hagan loosened the sword by his side. He'd greased the scabbard this morning, the sort of thing that's saved a man's life. Hagan sipped this second ale. Strange life. *I'm an exile. A…renegade.*

It hadn't sunk in. His departure from Morwella had been rushed. No time to dwell on niceties. Too busy dodging arrows, stealing boats, stowing away on merchantmen. *And here I am…*

Permio. A tavern, in the worst corner of a very bad city, Cappel Cormac. Hive of every cutthroat, cutpurse, and murderous whore imaginable. A place where, he, Hagan felt quite at home.

But he was angry. He felt wronged—they'd exiled him. The Duke, his people. *And for what?* A bit of raiding and robbing. Hagan the Highwayman. Hagan liked the thought of that. But it was the principle. The word *exile* tasted bad. Lacked honor. *I didn't deserve that.*

Others had done far worse and they hadn't suffered such a punishment. They'd been hanged, a few hung, drawn and quartered. But he'd been *exiled*—the dishonor was a stain on his family's name. Not that that mattered as they were all fucking dead. But the Delmorier family had once been wealthy merchants, before Hagan's grandfather had squandered every penny, except the few his only surviving son lost in the vice dens. Father choked on his ale one night—selfish bastard, served him right. Didn't leave much for the skinny boy he'd abandoned, Hagan's mother having left them years earlier.

He'd grown up poor—survived the streets of Vangaris. Had nothing except his family's name.

But a name was important. A name meant—*everything*. Until now. Way down here he was just another villain, another killer with a grudge.

Hagan sipped his second ale, his mood darkening as he thought about how they'd wronged him back there in the north. A thousand miles away. *I can never go back—see home again.*

Didn't matter, Morwella was a shithole anyway. Taxed and squeezed not only by lofty Duke Tomais, but by the High King over in Kella City.

At least he was free now. Almost spent of coin, no horse, no home—*but free.* Hagan smiled a third time. *It's becoming a habit.* Then turned his head as fighting broke out near the door.

The newcomers had rounded on those gang members at the table. Old score by the look of it, Hagan wasn't interested. Just glanced over, saw the bottle broken and rammed into the fat one's eye. *Messy, that.* Hagan, mood shifting again, chugged down his drink and stood up. He needed somewhere to sleep out the afternoon, and food. That too.

The fight settled almost as soon as it had started. Two dead on the floor, the fat one screaming as blood streamed from his ruined face. The gang had fled, the three big lads were seated at their table. They wore broadswords, Hagan noted. Northerners like him.

Mercenaries.

One glanced his way as Hagan waded through the crowd, smoke, and perfume of whores as he aimed for the door. That swung open again, creaking, the hot afternoon sun blinding Hagan for a moment.

A man stood there. Tall, long shaggy hair, and a huge sword

swung across his shoulder. He barreled in, clearing a space through to the taproom where Rezala still sweated and grumbled.

"You're banned," Hagan heard Rezala say. Glancing back, he saw Shaggy-Hair reach over and grab Rezala's collar. Not the innkeep's day.

"Shut up, and pour me a large one." The accent was odd but familiar. Another northerner. Hagan was intrigued, and he noted how the three big men at the table were also staring at this longswordsman. They looked angrier than before. And one reached for his blade. The tall fellow didn't notice; he was watching Rezala fill a tankard.

"Better enjoy that," Rezala said. "Last one you're getting."

Hagan saw the innkeep nod to the nearest mercenary.

"That him?" The sellsword asked. Rezala nodded. The longswordsman seemed oblivious, cradled his ale and sighed, as though he was sharing a tender moment with his lover, no one else around. Hagan wondered if he were soft in the head.

All three were on their feet. Big, angry, and well balanced. Confident. *Professionals.* They shoved sweaty bodies aside heading for the place where Shaggy-Hair was making love to his beer. Men grumbled and swore, the odd one spat. But they parted like palm leaves in summer storm letting the three large figures through.

Hagan scratched his face where a mosquito had bitten him. He hadn't cared about the earlier fracas, but was interested now. Why were these northerners here? And who did they work for? He needed to know, could be useful later.

"Outside." Hagan saw Rezala hint the door as the nearest mercenary stormed up behind Shaggy-hair. "Don't want another mess in here."

The man ignored him, and slowly slid his broadsword free for maximum effect, men parting either side to allow him room to swing.

"Put that back or I'll shove it up your arse," the accent was almost Morwellan. The lead mercenary paused, sword half out of scabbard, his fellows hustled close behind.

A mistake.

Shaggy-hair turned, and with a speed Hagan had seldom witnessed, slammed an open palm hard into the leading mercenary's face, cracking the small bone in his nose. He crumpled, sunk from view. The other two leaped forward.

And were knocked back.

Elbow to face, fist on balls, boot stamping on ankle. Shaggy-hair grinned as he grabbed the pair by their ears and slammed their heads together. They slid to join their comrade on the floor.

Shaggy-hair turned away and started on his ale again, ignoring the swarm of eyes and hostile glances.

"And you said *I* was drawing attention to myself," Hagan muttered to Rezala, who had glanced his way briefly before crouching low, whispering to a boy. Hagan watched the lad vanish out a back exit, the bright glare dazzling him a second time.

"Off to get the Watch I should imagine," Hagan said, as men resumed their seats, apart from the three sprawled on the floor. They showed no sign of moving any time soon.

"Expect so," Shaggy-Hair turned slowly and noticed Hagan for the first time. "Don't know you."

"Just arrived," Hagan said. "Think I'm going to like it here."

"No one likes it here," Shaggy-Hair said.

"Friends of yours?" Hagan hinted the three on the floor.

"Not really. They work for his boss," Shaggy-hair leaned over the counter, grabbed an empty tankard and hurled it at Rezala - catching him on the back of the head and knocking him from his feet.

He turned and grinned at Hagan. "I was banned anyway," he said, draining his tankard and striding from the room, a wave of bodies parting to let him through. Hagan suspected most had hands on daggers, and some would be following.

He chose to tag along.

"Wait," Hagan said, and the longsword stopped, turning slowly to stare hard at Hagan. *A man like me—a killer.* Someone with a grudge.

Steely eyes, the hue of northern oceans. Lean face, long bones, wicked scar above right brow. Black leather tunic and trousers. Silver studded belt, and battered mail shirt showing beneath.

"Name's Hagan Delmorier."

"Corin."

"From where—I can't grasp that accent."

"Fol—I'm Corin an Fol," he replied as though that were significant.

"Isn't that a province of Kelthaine?"

"Fuck off—it's a free country," the man called Corin said. "Nothing to do with Kelthaine, or the fucking High King."

"Sorry," Hagan shrugged. "Just curious."

"So are they," Corin said. Hagan turned and saw at least a dozen men had followed them out into the swelter of a Cappel Cormac afternoon. They stood in a circle surrounding Hagan and his new friend.

"I would leave if I were you," Corin said. "Me they want."

"I've only just arrived," Hagan yawned—past time for his afternoon nap. The stomp and scrape of boots in the distance, getting nearer. Shouting too. "Sounds like the Watch."

"Time I left," Corin said, and whirled around planting a fist neatly on the jaw of a bystander who'd got too near. He stepped sideways, slid the huge sword from its scabbard and shoved it point-first into the hot dry mud that served as a street in this shithole of a city.

The watch filed in looking nervous, tense, and very angry. "Your move," Corin said, flashing them a grin. They shuffled, glanced sideways at each other. A captain of sorts pushed his way through. Rezala yelled at him, holding a wet cloth to his bleeding skull.

"I barred him," Rezala said. "He's a troublemaker."

"All your punters are troublemakers," the captain looked pained, not wanting any of this. He pointed to Hagan. "And who is this?"

"I'm Hagan—just arrived."

"Well you'd better bugger off," the captain of the watch said. "Else we nab you for collusion."

"I only stepped out to enjoy the sunshine," Hagan said. No one was moving: captain, innkeep, the watch, tenants from the inn, and now bystanders and street vendors and even the odd, scarf covered whore—everyone had eyes on that two-yard sword, and the wild-eyed northerner leaning on it.

The captain approached Hagan, while staring at the other northerner. "I said go," the watch's leader hissed in Hagan's ear, then turned and yelled at his men. "Get him!"

Three spears levelled and poking, their owners thrust forward without too much enthusiasm. Bad mistake. *You have to do something properly, or not at all.* Hagan stepped away from the captain and blinked as metal glinted, there was a whoosh and a meaty thud. He saw a man's head rolling in the mud. A second joined it, then an arm.

"Time to run!" Corin shouted across to him.

Past time. Hagan turned on his toes, cat-graceful he pounced at the captain and kicked him in the groin, following up with an elbow to the face as the watch leader crumpled. Hagan grabbed an arm, swung the captain around into the next man attacking him. Both sprawled. Hagan saw Corin was loping down the street with that huge sword whirling like a windmill.

For fuck's sake… Thanks for waiting. Hagan stepped back, slid his rapier free and cut left and right. Swift clean strokes. They backed away. A gap appeared. He ran through just in time to see Corin vanish into a side street.

Two hours later they were in in another corner of town. Bells ringing, a chain of shabby shaven-headed priests chanting their way off to prayer. Hagan yawned.

Keep drinking—fend off sleep. He needed to learn the rules here. If there were any.

Another tavern. This one was empty, though no cleaner than Rezala's had been. Hagan guessed there wasn't a decent quarter to this city, or if there was it was well hidden.

He studied his new companion. Odd fellow. Tall and ungainly. Scary eyes— funny, they always said the same about Hagan himself. His own were slate gray, this Corin's flecked with winter blue. Long smoky-dark hair tied back, almost combed. He wore a cloak, pinned by a golden broach, a wolf's head stamped upon it—almost aristocratic. *Stolen?* Hagan smiled. *We could pass for brothers.*

"Safe here," Corin grinned at him as a girl glided close and placed a hot dish of rice and beans, and, *was that chicken?* Before them at the table. Corin tucked in. Hagan stared at the food and realized he hadn't eaten since he'd jumped off that ship this morning. It smelled wonderful. He took a bite. Spicy, hot.

"Silon's place," Corin said, glancing up and blowing a kiss at the girl who grinned lopsidedly and vanished into the kitchens.

"Who?"

"Boss," Corin munched.

"Pay well?"

"Hope so—only been working for him a month. Down here the whole time."

Hagan looked up. "So, your boss ain't from here then."

"Fuck no," Corin laughed though Hagan failed to see what was funny. "Silon hates Permians—especially those in this city."

"Where's he from then?"

"Raleen," Corin said, his eyes on the girl who had reappeared with two large mugs of ale. The fourth round since they'd arrive. "Atarios—though he owns a villa near Port Sarfe too. Minted."

"Sounds like it."

"Met him during the war," Corin said before Hagan could ask. "Helped me out with a personal issue, then persuaded me to work for him."

"Doing what?"

"A little light dusting." The laugh again. Strange sense of humor.

"Does he need a second sellsword?"

"I can ask."

"Thanks—I'm between jobs," Hagan said.

"Last one didn't pay well, by the looks of you," Corin picked up his plate and poured rice into his mouth. He belched and wiped his hands on his shirt, already grimy from the fight before.

Hagan felt his face redden as anger rose. "It's a sore point," he said. "I come from noble stock."

Corin shrugged. "None of my business."

"That's right," Hagan said. He managed a crooked smile. "You weren't to know. I'm a wanted man way up in Morwella."

"And in Permio," Corin grinned.

"Those louts?"

"That captain will have bleated to the Elite by now," Corin said. "The sultan's special boys. Crimson-cloaked tosspots. They don't like us northerners—despite us saving their ruler from assassination several times."

"Who were those three toughs?" Hagan said. "Looked like ex Regiment lads."

"Bears," Corin said, fingering the gold brooch and scowling.

"Ah," Hagan was surprised to discover himself smiling yet again. "And you were a Wolf—under the late Lord Halfdan?"

"Late?" Corin's eyes were sharp as daggers and locked on Hagan.

"Murdered—or so they say—by Lord Caswallon," Hagan felt slightly unsettled under that scrutiny. Not like him to get unnerved by another's gaze, but there was a raw savageness, almost a hunger in Corin's eyes.

"A rumor I heard," Hagan said dismissively. "Tavern talk."

"I don't believe it," Corin said, and called across to the girl for more beer.

"So, what's with you and those Bears?" Hagan knew of the famous rivalry between the three royal regiments in Kelthaine. The Bears, the Wolves, and the High King's favorites, the Tigers, were all fiercely competitive.

"They're sultan's men," Corin spat on the floor.

"You said the sultan hates northerners."

"I know what I said—they fight well, and he pays well. Uses the twats to round up other decent folk."

"I didn't think there were any decent folk down here."

"Diminishing fast," Corin said. "They're fucking traitors, Hagan. We fought a war down here…good people died in that desert, and now these… ex-Bears side with the man responsible. Just for coin."

"I thought that's what mercenaries do," Hagan said. He didn't know the politics down here, but had timed his arrival poorly, the war with the desert tribes having ended scarce two months ago. A war he could have got lost in.

"Us and them," Corin said. "You work with Permians, not for them. Those boys crossed the line. I'll kill them one day."

"So why are you down here?" Hagan asked. "Why not guarding your wealthy merchant up in Atarios."

"Silon has investments in Cappel Cormac," Corin said. "He owns four coffee houses and this tavern. He likes to keep an eye on things down here, got his grubby nubbins in lots of pies."

"Sounds busy."

"I know Cappel," Corin said. "Was stationed here in the war.

Sprawling city, no shortage of hide outs. There's a man called Krugan, owes Silon money. Lots of money." Corin drained his beer. "Local villain, operates south of the city."

"Need a helping hand?"

"No," Corin said. "Got this. Silon wants Krugan watched. He thinks the man's a spy for the sultan, posing as a gang leader. Things are complex down here."

"Seems so." Hagan was about to enquire further when the girl rushed into the taproom, her dark eyes huge with fear.

"What is it, Letti?" Corin reached for his massive sword, and Hagan grabbed the hilt of his own weapon.

"Elite," she said. "Coming this way. Grolly the kitchen lad spotted them at market. He ran back to tell me."

"Good lad," Corin said. "Best we spread."

"I thought you said we'd be safe here?"

"We ought to be," Corin stole across to a backroom, Hagan followed close behind. "Someone must have followed us."

"We ran for an hour," Hagan said, helping Corin break through the mud wall that opened on the stables. "Switching from street to street." Hagan kicked a fist-sized hole in the wall. "This city's huge—we must have lost them?"

Corin shrugged and pitched his long body into the wall, it crumpled and Hagan slammed against it again, the pair crashing into the stables as the sound of shouts and heavy steel-shod boots entered the taproom behind.

"Grab a nag," Corin's face loomed out the murk. Dark and hot in the stable. "We'll make for the Strand," he said.

"The what?" Hagan, eyes slowly adjusting to the dark, saw Corin vault onto the back of a pony.

"Yah!" He reared the beast and it kicked out knocking the doors asunder.

Hagan blinked. He saw a torch, helmets appearing from behind the collapsed wall.

No fucking saddle…

He leaped onto something—hoped it was a horse. A sword whooshed through air behind him. Hagan dug his heels in and the pony cantered out into the late evening gloom.

He crouched low over the pony's head, heard the sound he dreaded. Arrows whining, then thudding into mud and buildings as Hagan hollered at the beast to pick up its pace. There was no sign of Corin an Fol. *Thanks for sticking by me, Longfellow.*

Hagan made the docks. Dismounted, forced a fisher at sword point take him onboard and cut the bowline.

Hours later, dark and silent, stars studding the black above, the skiff beached on a sandy shore. Hagan leaped from the craft, tossed his last coin to the fisher by way of compensation and strode up toward the distant shadow of palms.

He was outside the city, penniless, exhausted and bruised. He staggered towards the line of palms, the beach gleaming white below his feet, and all around. A silent empty world, but for the sigh and surge of waves. Hagan collapsed beneath the shelter of the nearest palm tree and sprawled face-first in the sand.

His last thought was that when next he saw Corin an Fol he'd gut him open with a blunt knife.

Chapter 2 | Summoned

Wind in his hair, hot sun blazing down, and dolphins dancing ahead of the prow. The ship tossing and pitching as blue waves mustered. Corin grinned; he loved the sea—his heritage, the future stolen from him.

I should have been a fisher like my kin.

But those kin were dead, all save the one sister lost somewhere in the deep desert. Father, mother, brothers, younger sister— all gone. And the girl he'd loved—Holly—a fading memory of another time. What war did to a man.

He'd seen twenty-seven summers. Over ten years since he'd been home. Fighting in foreign wars. Blood, death, and betrayal. Losing friends and lovers. Such a life offers two choices: die or grow stronger. Corin chose the latter course.

Six days at sea gives you time to think. Not necessarily a good thing. Memories, like ghosts stalk at night. Sleepless, tossing in the bunk. Faces of people he'd known, loved. Fought alongside, against. All gone, and yet flashing back in those dark lonely moments. *Not enough ale.*

Corin forced a grin, determined to make the most of this voyage. He was what he was. Been made that way by fate, the gods, or just bad luck. No point dwelling on it. *Take each day as it comes.* They'd make harbor this afternoon, already a thin line hinted cliff to the north. *Raleen—his new home.* A fresh start.

It hadn't gone well thus far.

Silon had sent him south to stake out this Krugan character. But a task like that takes time—especially in Permio. In Cappel Cormac a false step resulted in death. One careless whisper or too much ale and you're rat food, rotting in a gutter. He'd followed steps, asked questions when he'd dared. Got the whereabouts of Krugan's camp. Then that shit with the Bears had happened in the *Crimson Moon.* Nothing untoward. Shit always happened to Corin an Fol.

But someone had followed Corin and the Morwellan. Stalked them across the city. *Who? Why…?* In Cappel Cormac no one cared, even the Sultan's Elite could be bribed. Corin knew that city—every grubby nook and corner. He'd been careful; Hagan the Morwellan had too.

But someone had outplayed them, which sent warning signals up Corin's spine. The Elite had found Silon's safe house. That should not have happened. Got to report back to the new boss. *Someone is on to us.*

"We'll dock in a couple of hours," Dol Craile the fisher's skipper told him. Whip lean with ebony skin, large golden earring in left ear. Scarred, artful, and dangerous, the skipper worked for Silon too. Covertly of course. Corin liked him, though Craile had trounced him at dice every night.

"Thanks," Corin said to the skipper, turning to face the bow again. The dolphins were leaving, dancing and leaping off to port. Corin watched them go, a sweeping sadness stealing his moment.

Yazrana—he'd lost her too. His lover during the war. The tough Permian lass who'd taught him how to use a longsword. The best fighter he'd known. Butchered in that raid. Betrayed by that bastard Taskala, the Regiment's Swordmaster who'd almost got Corin hanged. The man he'd killed on Gardale Moor.

Again, he shut out those memories. *I need a drink...* He'd stop by the *Crooked Knife* for a few ales before making north to Atarios. He'd be there by the end of the week—no rush. Bad news could wait.

Corin wondered how the Morwellan —Hagan— fared. Unlikely he'd survived. Shame, but the man should have kept up. You couldn't hesitate in Permio. Had to keep moving.

Corin's gaze shifted to the sky above where three white birds glided north toward the distant shoreline. Raleen, most southerly of the Four Kingdoms. Fiercely independent and proud. Descendants of the warrior Kael who'd escaped the ruin of Gol. So, the stories went. Not that Corin cared overmuch.

Those cliffs were bigger and Corin could just discern the vast Liaho Delta over to his right, a shimmering haze. Somewhere beyond that was Port Sarfe, Dol Craile's current home. Though Skipper Craile was no Raleenian. He came from Yamondo or Vendel, lands Corin knew little about in the distant south.

"'Moved here when things got too hot,'" Dol Craile had told Corin, and explained that his country had been at war with its neighbor for decades. Places south of the desert, Corin hadn't listened. Didn't care.

They docked as afternoon sun spilled yellow on the quayside. Port Sarfe. Corin remembered the first time he'd come here. A green angry youth—untried, and untested, but filled with fire in his belly. And wanting revenge. Forlorn hope that had proved. He'd sought news of his sister Ceilyn, taken by raiders. That search had led to a deserted graveyard, hinting an echo of her footsteps vanishing into the vastness of the Permian Desert. A trail turned cold. Leaving no marks for him to follow.

Enough!

Corin vaulted from the vessel after parting with coin and shaking on the deal. Dol Craile was leaving in the morning, just a quick turnaround for his crew. Sell, restock, hit the taverns, and then away before sun up. Not a bad life, in Corin's opinion.

He walked briskly along the harbor ignoring the bustle: shouting, curses, laughs, dogs barking, the stink of rotting fish, whores' cheap scents, horse shit, and tanneries away in the distance. Corin strolled without hindrance. Most folk knew to steer clear of this scar-faced northerner with the huge sword strapped to his back.

Corin reached the *Crooked Knife*, his preferred tavern, stepped through the door and took seat at table, lips salivating at the smells coming from the kitchens close by. *Good to be back...*

The inn was quiet, between late and early, that lull when folk napped or finished up their tasks by the quayside. The landlord— Rado—was busy in the yard. Portly and genial, and one of the few Raleenians Corin trusted. The innkeep nodded, hinted he'd be over in a moment. Corin waited, unfastened Clouter from his back, slid the blade free and commenced oiling the five-foot steel with his rag.

"I'd sooner you'd stow that monstrosity," Rado said. "It'll upset my customers."

Corin glanced around. "I don't see any customers," but he complied and slid Clouter back in its scabbard. "Needed something to do. Things on my mind."

"Haven't we all," Rado said, taking brief seat opposite Corin at table. "Tashi will bring a jug over in a nonce."

"Tashi?"

"New girl," Rado said. "Good lass—bright, sharp tongue. Don't know why she's here—could do much better up in the city."

Footsteps approaching, stealthy and soft. Corin turned, smiled at the girl coming his way. Short, slim, and neat. Sleek black hair tied neatly back. Pale skin—unusual for Raleenians. Dark eyes. She wore a confident easy smile and walked with a feline grace. Not your average tavern wench.

Without a word the girl placed the jug of ale on the table. She glanced briefly at Corin, those canny eyes hinted irony and humor. Lost on him. But not that body. The slim hips, the way she seemed to glide. Rado was right. The girl was wasted here.

"Got a note for you."

"What?" Corin was still looking at the doorway Tashi had breezed through, hoping she'd return in a moment. Best sight he'd seen in weeks.

"A letter from Silon. I know his seal."

"He's written a note—for me?" Corin realized his mouth was open and slammed it shut in case Tashi returned and thought him a halfwit.

"I'll go get it," Rado said. "The man said you'd be arriving today."

"What man?" Corin felt a flash of irritation. How could Silon or anyone else know he was back in Raleen? Something untoward was happening here. Rado reappeared and dropped a rolled parchment on the table. Vellum. Expensive and rare, and that seal unmistakable. The 'S' surrounded by a five-pointed star.

Corin stared at the note as though it were a viper. "You not going to open it?" Rado said.

"I need a moment," Corin said.

"Say no more," Rado said, and shuffled off into the kitchens. Corin, annoyed, glanced up as two sailors entered the *'Knife*. One nodded his way but Corin ignored them. He stared at the note.

Fuck it. Corin slipped his hunting knife out and cut through the seal. The words were written bold and clear in the merchant's elaborate hand.

I will expect you at Vioyamis this evening. Do not delay. S.

"Doesn't make sense," Corin grumbled as he reread the note. The girl— Tashi—returned and replenished the jug but Corin hardly noticed her this time. She glided away, and Rado returned.

"Good news?"

"Buggered if I know," Corin said. "Probably bad. Where or what is Vioyamis?"

"Silon's villa," Rado looked shocked. "You've not been there?"

"Never heard of it."

"Oh…well, it's a landmark for most Raleenians. Few people have that kind of money."

"Vioyamis is in Sarfe? A house?"

"A mansion, villa, or castle…? I've not seen it up close," Rado said. "It's in the countryside fifteen miles inland. Can't miss it. Stands on a hill surrounded by vineyards, and woods. The walls the color of alabaster. Kelwynian marble. Glows like a fallen star in sunset. Named after a nymph or something."

"A what?"

"You'd better leave right away," Rado said.

"Why should I—just got here?"

"I know Silon," Rado said. "If he summoned you then you need to attend sharp—see what he wants. Could be a pay rise?"

"More likely the heave-ho," Corin drained his mug and stood up. "But I take your point, Rado. Besides, I want to find out what the fuck is going on. Silon wanted me in Permio for another month at least. How could he know I was coming back?"

"That merchant has his ways," Rado smiled.

"Spies, you mean," Corin grumbled, and fastened Clouter to his back again. "Be seeing you," he nodded to Rado and made for the door. He stopped when Tashi glided across his path.

"You ride into peril, Corin an Fol," she said softly so only he could hear. "Have a care, and watch your back." She smiled in an infuriatingly knowing way, and then disappeared back into the kitchens.

"What?" Corin shouted after her and then stormed outside into the late afternoon heat.

Next time I'll put a fucking flag up announcing arrival.

Corin stormed through the harbor, his face as long as the day. He reached a lane, turned into the city main. His long strides pacing up pavements until he saw the barbican ahead. Silon's private stables were adjacent. The merchant had six thoroughbreds kept in prime condition for himself and guests. One reserved for Corin an Fol. He'd expected to come here tonight and ride north to the capital, Atarios. A four days ride stopping at taverns and taking his ease. Not to be.

He was curious though. And angry. And what was with that girl? *'You ride into peril.'* Where had he heard that before?

A rudderless boat, driven willy-nilly by random tide, Corin felt confused, and varying emotions tossed this way and that. A quick chat followed at the stables. The stable guard and duty boy had the horse waiting. No great surprise. Corin vaulted on the mare's back and the guards let him out the city without so much as a grunt.

A fallen star. Fifteen miles inland near the road to South Kaelin, the disputed border region above Permio. *Can't miss it.*

A dusty canter saw Corin arriving on a ridge awarding wide views east over dry hills, open valleys, and the odd stub of brush. Raleen was half desert this far south, which was why the villa stood out. White marble reflected by the sun. Blazing—a fallen star indeed. The glare dazzled him even from this distance.

Corin shielded his eyes with a hand and studied the villa. White, sprawling, and stately. Wrapped by woods, standing high on a flat round hill. A statement more than a home. Corin hated the place at first sight. Stone-faced, he road toward it, urging the mare pick up pace.

The green foliage coating the hill's flanks was remarkable, surrounded by all that yellow below, the brush, arid hills, and the desert border not far to the south. Corin slowed his horse to a walk as he weaved through woods, and then vineyards neatly lined in rows, men and women busy everywhere he looked.

A retainer met him in the gardens, a groom following close behind. Corin slid off his horse and the groom led the beast away. He hardly noticed, or even listened as the retainer told him to seek the merchant in his private lobby.

Corin surveyed the gardens as he strolled through, seeing statues, lawns the hue of fresh cut emeralds, fountains chiming like pipe music, diverted streams, palms swaying in breeze, figs laden with fruit, and tall cedars rising like jade towers reaching for the sun. Enough to dazzle a fighting man's head.

He reached an avenue of olive trees, a pergola thrust within, vines and clematis, and deep red roses trailing amongst it. Ahead were wide doors leading into the villa proper. Another servant met him there, garbed in immaculate white with gold hems.

"Take off your boots," the man said.

"What?" Corin complied after a moment's gawping about. The villa was vast—a maze. Halls led into rooms, and these opened on further halls. A man could get lost in here. Everywhere were urns, busts of gods, demigods, and long dead heroes. Inch thick carpets and rugs smoothed the way for his socks, and ornate lighting spilled subtle gold and silver, the arched windows veiled by drapes screening the hot Raleen sun.

Corin reached a door. The servant stepped forward and tapped three times.

"Enter." The servant stepped back and nodded Corin go in.

"It's me," Corin said as he stepped inside Silon's office. "I'm back." He glanced around, not seeing the merchant. He did see books, parchments, maps on walls showing lands he'd never heard of. Paintings of weird beasts, ancient battles, and one of a beautiful foreign-looking woman. Corin like that one. A desk, multicolored carpets, three large windows looking out over shaded gardens and distant hills beyond. Facing west. As he watched the sun was setting red-gold above those hills and flooding copper into the room.

"Sit." Corin glanced around, noticed the top of a shaven head above another desk over to his right. A table stood beside it. Two chairs, a crystal decanter half-filled with rose-colored wine. Two glasses.

Corin pulled up a chair and yawned. The day was proving a challenge to his senses. "I'm back," he said again for want of anything better.

Silon placed the large map he was studying on the desk in from of him and sighed. He rubbed his neat hands on a white towel and reached forward offering the second glass to Corin.

"You'll need that."

Corin sipped. The wine was excellent of course, but wasted on him. Wine was for merchants, lords, and fancy folk. Beer was his preferred beverage. That said this was a finely delicate liquid. He swiveled the glass and belched. Silon just looked at him.

"I had to abort," Corin said. "We were betrayed."

"You were careless," Silon said, his gaze flicking to a gardener raking leaves outside.

"No, I was unlucky," Corin said. "Spent a deal of time and effort laying down traps, getting information, only to get—"

"I don't need excuses," Silon said. "I've a more immediate matter requiring your...skills." Corin studied the merchant's face. Lean, hard, and needle-sharp, the stubble of white whiskers covering head and face. The gold-mounted diamond studding his left ear. That crafty brown gaze. *So Raleenian.* The narrow mouth and firm set jaw, frown lines cutting into deep tan.

"We're being played," Silon said, rolling the crystal glass deftly in his fingers. "A man wants me dead."

Corin shrugged. "Most people I've met want me dead," he said.

"That's understandable," Silon said, "considering what you do. But I've some intricate work that's had me sailing closer to the rocks than is comfortable.

"You have a boat too?"

"Yes, you moron—but I was being metaphorical."

"Oh…"

Silon rolled his eyes and gazed out the window again. the gardener saw him looking and made himself scarce. Corin wiped sweat from his sleeve and yawned again. "Will this take long?" he said.

"An arrow nearly found me in Atarios," Silon said. "A black arrow. A warning, I realize that now."

"Shot by whom?" Corin drained the wine glass, at last he was interested. His kind of conversation.

"An archer," Silon said. He smiled briefly, "Joke." Corin nodded. *Not your strong point.* "There was a note glued to the shaft."

Another fucking note…

"What did it say," Corin said leaning forward at the table.

"'Twas plainly written," Silon said. "'*I can reach you whenever I need to. You cannot hide from me,*'" —that's all."

"A boast?" Corin flicked his glance to the window where the copper light was fading slowly. Quiet and serene out there, the trees swaying slightly in late summer breeze. A pale moon rising claimed territory deserted by the stolen sun, silver light filtered down through trees. Corin felt a shiver. A memory. Another woman. Her eyes of green and gold.

"Are you listening?"

"I was thinking," Corin said looking at the merchant.

"Don't do that," Silon said. He poured another glass of wine and took a sip. "Three acquaintances of mine were murdered in Kelthaine last month. Kella City to be precise."

"Dangerous place," Corin said. "Only been there once. I left in a hurry the next day."

"Skewered by a black arrow," Silon said. "The poison left them screaming for hours. Not a good way to go."

"No indeed. Who were these people?"

"Merchants," Silon said. "Contacts, and the last one a dear old friend."

"I'm sorry," Corin said. "And you think you're next?"

"No, it's worse than that. As I said that arrow was a warning. The assassin is working for someone who wants to divert me from my private business up north. A powerful player. Killing me out of hand leaves questions unanswered for him. He doesn't like riddles— a master conniver. This player wants to scare me and corner me and hurt what's mine. Cause me to panic and spill my secrets. Hence the hunt and the taunting words. The silent stalker."

"Well I'm here now," Corin said folding his arms. "I'll stake out the villa, set snares on the paths, and murder anything bigger than a bunny."

"The threat isn't here," Silon said. "It's up in Atarios. I need you there."

"I can't protect you if I'm up there."

"I'm not talking about me," Silon said. He looked uncomfortable, vulnerable even. A rare look for him. Corin had a sinking feeling.

Fuck...

"Nalissa?"

"Yes," Silon sighed. "I need you to go fetch her."

Nalissa...

Chapter 3 | The Killer

Two hundred miles north the evening bells were tolling and the devout were strolling toward the temple of Elanion. Nalissa watched them from her balcony, wondering what it was like to be a good citizen. Not that she had much interest in worship. Boring. The Goddess didn't care about her, so why should she care back?

Parties, functions. These were Nalissa's favorite diversions. Life was for living after all. Not for her the drab meaningless continuation of toil, prayer and monotony. She needed excitement. Stimulation. Nalissa needed *fun*.

It was in short supply at the moment. Their town house was her prison. Her father had ridden south, tight-lipped and tense, leaving her with dry Uncle Rubain, who never had a good word for her. And had accused her father of doting on her. *To think of it!*

She stamped her foot. Waved the empty wine glass at those silly people out there. She'd call out and get a servant to replenish. Next thing, Uncle Rubain would be confiscating that. It had been a long summer, even hotter than usual. Long and so bloody boring. The last party was weeks ago. How they'd fussed over her dress that night.

Nalissa crinkled her nose at the memory. *Poor fools—all vying for my hand and father growling at them from the corner.* But Nalissa didn't care a fig about any of them. They were boring too. Predictable and pointless.

But there was one man who had pricked her curiosity. A dangerous man who'd excited her several months back. Down there in the gardens, she'd been very indiscreet. *If father knew...*

Nalissa tossed her head spilling those long wavy locks around her face. She pictured that man's rough face in her mind, and again felt his rougher hands poring over her body. A tingle, she smiled. A lot of fun that night.

Where was Corin now?

"I need more wine," Nalissa shoved her hand out and somebody took her glass away. Moments later it was placed back in her hand, her long fingers wrapping around. "Thank you," she remembered to say, her eyes on the streets below. Empty now.

A soft sound behind her. The servant?

"What is it?" Nalissa said, and then coughed and choked as the gloved hand covered her mouth and iron-strong fingers twisted her arm so the glass dropped, smashing to shards on the patio below.

She couldn't scream, the gloved hands had her pinned and trussed. A calm voice spoke to her right. Nalissa glimpsed a woman standing on the balcony beside her. A pale-faced woman with an ironic smile on her face. She looked foreign, dangerous, clad in black faded leather. A curved sword at her hip.

"Be gentle with her," the woman said, her voice was husky. "We'll get a good price for this one."

Nalissa stamped her foot down hard catching her captor's toe. He coughed, for an instant his grip loosened and she sank her molars into his hand.

"Fuck!" The voice growled in her ear. Nalissa elbowed him in the belly and made a jump for it. The man followed, a backward glance had her seeing him clearly. Big, ugly, clad in shabby leather, gloves and boots—all dirty sooty and stained.

"Fuck off!" Nalissa had her knife out and jabbed it toward him.

Father always insisted she kept a blade close to ward off chancers. The man hesitated, looked across to the woman who was smiling.

"What's so funny?" Nalissa spat at the woman and then flicked her knife up at her accomplice, inching toward her, his arms outstretched. "Get back, villain!" Nalissa spat. "Do you know who I am?"

"Oh yes," the woman said smiling still. "That's the reason we're here." She approached Nalissa's left as the man reached for her again. Nalissa jabbed with her knife but the woman was quicker, her own hidden blade shot past Nalissa's head in a flash of silver and stuck in the man's neck.

He choked, coughed blood, and slunk to the ground, thrashing for a few seconds before laying still, his dead glazed eyes staring up at Nalissa. She made to scream but the woman placed a pale finger on her lips, the nail painted a deep midnight blue. The sight made her shudder inside

"Shush, darling," the killer said. "Let's do this right. I need your cooperation—better for you."

"You…killed him," Nalissa's eyes were locked on that dead face like a deer trapped and cornered, the horror slowly sinking in. Blood oozing from his neck, dripping from the balcony. A fascinatingly revolting sight.

"He was clumsy," the woman said. "Unprofessional. I cannot work with idiots."

"Who are you?" Nalissa turned her face from the horror and stared at the woman. Pale and slender, poised like a dancer. Confident. Her eyes like chips of shiny wet coal. And something else. A shadow of menace lurking beneath that gaze that made Nalissa's guts churn.

"We need to leave," the woman's smile was persuasive, comradely even. "Two horses wait outside the gates, and a boat awaits morning tide at Kador Docks."

"I'm not going," Nalissa stood her ground, leveled the knife at this terrible woman. "My uncle…the servants–"

"Are no more."

Uncle…

"Sorry about that," the killer said. "I have to keep things tidy, no loose ends. Mistakes can find a nice girl dead."

"Well dead you fucking are!" Nalissa jabbed the knife at the woman's eyes. The swipe went wide, and steel-strong hands twisted the blade from her fingers, followed swiftly by a fist battering the side of her face. Nalissa sprawled to her knees and the woman kicked her in the mouth, splitting her lip.

Nalissa sobbed and looked up. The woman stood over her. That easy smile had departed, replaced by a cold cruel stare, like the last day of autumn swallowed by unannounced blizzard. Those eyes coolly surveyed her dispassionately, much as an eagle or hawk studies its kill, the talons on the brink of tear.

"Get up," the woman said at last. "On your feet, and I hope you've learnt your lesson. Nobody fucks with me, girl—understood?"

Nalissa nodded, her sobs subsiding to a frosty realization that her life had taken a turn for the worse. "I-"

"Didn't want to hurt you," the woman leaned forward and wiped blood from Nalissa's mouth. "Shame, and I'll have to stitch that up, but it won't stop you pleasuring a man—or woman," she smiled at some private joke.

"Now, I need you to walk," the woman said. "Arm in arm with me to the city gates. The guards won't trouble us—I paid them good coin."

"What do you want with me?" Nalissa said fighting back the tears.

"Nothing," the woman answered. "This is a contract, and you, sweet thing, are going to make me rich."

***

Blood covering his hands and agony in his side, Rubain of Atarios crawled to the gatehouse, shouted, his voice raw and hoarse. No one out there. He tried again, heard the patter of tiny footsteps. A small boy stood gaping.

"Get help," Rubain said, and then gasped as the pain tore into him again. The boy stared at him in silence. "Go." Rubain blacked out. When he came to a face hovered over him. A hard face going in and out of focus. Rubain tried to speak, leaned over and spewed on the floor. He lay in a bed the pain in his side tearing up at him, but he was alive. Better than he'd expected.

The face loomed, another person hovered behind. Rubain half recognized one of the servants—Rosa. He smiled faintly happy she lived.

"We were raided." He couldn't remember their faces. Only sudden pain— agony, and a heaviness in his side and someone laughing softly. *A woman?* "I need to get up."

"Rest," the rough face above him broke into a scowl. "You need to rest."

Suddenly Rubain tensed in horror. "Nalissa?"

"Taken." The face backed away and Rubain heard boots scraping in the hallway. Rosa leaned over him.

"You're badly hurt, Sir," Rosa said. *Sweet kind Rosa — so happy you're alive.* "You must do as he says, get your strength back."

"Who?" Rubain's vision was blurring again.

"Him." She jerked her head disapprovingly but the other face had vanished. "The mercenary, the northerner. He arrived this morning."

"How long have I been here?"

"Four days. We thought we'd lost you." She smiled and wiped tears from her eyes.

"You survived—I'm happy."

"I wasn't here, it was my day off," she said. "That boy found me and I brought the Watch. But the villains were long gone, save one dead in Nalissa's courtyard.

"They took her?"

"Must have," Rosa flicked her face hinting the pacing sound in the hallway outside. "He says he'll get her back." She didn't sound confident.

"What about...?"

"They're all dead, Rat the cook, the Dyer sisters. Everyone. I can't get over it. Blood everywhere, we found you lying by the gate in the street. Flies covering you." She'd started weeping.

"There now," Rubain said. "We'll get her back— it's most likely money they want." He wanted to say more but the blackness returned and the world faded into nothingness.

***

Corin left the wounded man and maid servant to their mutual misery. He needed air, so stormed up the stairs and crashed into Nalissa's room, forcing open the expensive glass doors and reaching the balcony—her favorite place, apparently.

Too fucking late.

By a rat's whisker he'd arrived too late. The City Watch had already sent word south. Silon would be murderous. Corin had ridden like a man possessed, squeezing a four-day journey into two very long ones. But still he'd arrived too late. He kicked a vase from a small round table knocking it out to the street below. Angry didn't cover it.

I need to think. Where would they have taken her? How many? He had already examined the corpse. A common cutthroat by the looks, and known to the Watch. Expendable. Not part of the bigger plan. Throat sliced wide open. *Must have gotten greedy.*

Corin wiped sweat from his face and stared down at the city

below. What to do? They'd found Silon's brother two days ago. Corin doubted he'd last the night but Rubain defied the Crow Gatherer yet. Tough old bugger. Corin felt a new respect for him. Didn't know him well and hadn't much cared for what he did know.

What to do…?

He heard feet, turning saw the older woman, Rosa, standing at the doorway to the balcony. "He's lost consciousness again," she said, her expression more than a little hostile. *This one doesn't like me.* "What are you going to do?"

"Get her back," Corin said matching the woman's tense glance until she turned away. "First I need to know what happened here."

"They were robbers," she said, as though it were obvious. "Master Rubain must have tried fighting them off and even killed that one. Why they murdered everyone else. They must have panicked and fled. Didn't take anything—only her."

"That was why they came," Corin said. "You can go now."

The woman glared at him and then nodded.

"And you better start doing your job," she said and left him to his scrutiny.

Corin examined the dried blood, the scuff marks on the stone, a broken fingernail by the railing. She'd put up a fight. He smiled at the thought. That lass wouldn't have gone easy. Then he saw it. A rough sketch on the wall, carved by a knife point.

A mark left for whomever was tasked to clean up. Corin stooped low. The words were written below the table on the wall, not surprising he hadn't seen them. Scraped by a blade, they were hard to discern but he got their meaning easily enough. Four words followed by his name:

You ride into peril…Corin an Fol…

Then Corin noticed something else. *What was that—a cat?* An animal face, looked like a cat's carved into the wall, inches above the words. There was writing here too.

I am always ahead of you—the words written beside it.

Corin stood, stretched and wiped sweat from his face again. He pictured a pale face, a girl's wry smile, then the image left him. He took out his knife and stabbed it into the wall scraping away the words and the animal face.

"You have the advantage for the moment," Corin said to himself as he scraped. "But I'll get you." He walked back into the town house ignoring Rosa's critical eye. He found the wine cellar, uncorked a bottle and strolled out into the garden's, his thoughts on the last—the only time he'd been here before. The night Nalissa danced. *The night she and he…* The night Silon had taken him on.

He sat at a bench drinking from the bottle, allowing his tired head to clear, and his mind to gather what thoughts it could. Rosa appeared, but he ignored her.

'He doesn't pay you to drink," she said, standing fists on hips a few feet away.

"It helps me focus," Corin said. "Make yourself useful and get me some supper. I'm leaving within the hour."

"You know where they went?"

"Nope."

"Then why go when you can help the Watch scour this city?"

"Because whoever did this is no longer in this city, woman." She glared at him and Corin pulled a face. He really could do with some support. Even a smile would be encouraging. *No chance.* "He'll be making for the coast, her abductor," Corin said.

"Port Sarfe is miles away," Rosa said.

"Not Sarfe—Kador."

"That's even further."

"I know where it is," he passed the bottle across. Rosa stared at it for a moment and then shrugged. She took a long hard swig and then sat on the bench beside him. "Kador's smaller than Sarfe and less policed," Corin said. "They'll be looking for passage south. You can get a good price for a woman that comely in Permio."

"You think they were slavers?" Rosa looked horrified. "In Atarios?"

"No," Corin said. "This is one individual. A pro. Someone getting at Silon and paid to make him suffer. This killer's taking her south. I'm certain of it. Going to flog that poor lass to a Permian camel-shagger, and send word up to your boss of her suffering."

"Then you had better follow, mercenary," Rosa said, her former hostility had faded, replaced by a weary smile. "You're our only hope now."

"Name's Corin an Fol," he said, standing up and leaving her with the bottle. "And I'll get her back."

"You had better," Rosa said and drained the bottle. He left her looking dreamily into the bushes.

Half hour later as light fled the day, Corin had traded horses and left the walls of Raleen's first city behind, lost in a trail of dust, the moon riding above him and early stars studding the darkening sky.

Chapter 4 | The Green Duck

Keep your head down and keep moving. Never sleep in the same gutter twice. Sleep with one eye open, is best. *Dangerous city—but I'm a dangerous man.* Hagan opened an eye. Voices in the distance. Somewhere closer, cats screeching in an alley. He wrapped the old blanket around his body—surprising how chilly it got at night when it was so bloody hot during the daylight hours.

He'd slept on that beach for half a day, grubbed for sandworms, snails and lice—anything to fill his belly. That gave him enough strength to crawl back into the city. He'd found the old blanket discarded in the midden dumps, alongside rotting corpses, rats, and awful screeching birds who'd eyed him evilly.

It wasn't a disguise as he felt like the beggar he resembled, shuffling through the gates at dawn, cursed by guards, cowing under the rotten food and stones they tossed his way.

Bastards

Hagan had lurked in the docks until nightfall. There was always a place for beggars in the docks. He'd eaten scraps, killed a dog when it got too close. Being hungry gave a man an edge, but it also weakened you. Hagan didn't like feeling weak. A week passed. He hung on, getting slowly stronger. And angrier.

I need a plan—a project. Reason to stay alive.

The whole world hated him, gods, men—even dogs. Fuck the lot of them. Hagan didn't care. *You fall this far, things get simple. You either die or life improves.* Hagan wasn't planning on dying anytime soon.

He still had his rapier secreted under the cloak, a knife too. Tools for survival. Rats scurried through garbage in the alley. Night sounds in the city. Someone coughed, a rasping awful croak, and further away he heard a woman cry out in rapture. Closer, a window opened and a man tossed a bowl of shit out into the cut, the contents splashed Hagan's face. He hardly blinked; he was stinking enough already.

Dawn came. The red sun rising, and welcome heat warming his aching bones. And the return of the stench. Hagan had never smelled anything like this city. Shithole didn't cover it. He staggered to his feet. *Back to the docks?* No, he decided on another course. He needed to learn the layout of the city, and what made it work.

Every city has its order no matter how chaotic. Even this place must have laws. The sultan had his spies, those elite tossers in the red cloaks, the city watch, the gate guards—all desperate to fuck up someone's day. Then there were the foreigners, merchants mostly, and fighting men like him. Though he hadn't the strength for a fight this morning.

Hagan staggered, stretched, and clambered through the garbage until he found a wider alley leading deeper into the city. He shuffled for an hour, blanket over face hiding his northern features. Limping, he'd found a cup and held it up whenever someone got close. They spat at him, several kicked, and one man stabbed out with his blade. That one died in a deserted alley.

Hagan stooped over the corpse. Big brute, most likely some local bully boy. Wasn't going to hurt anyone with his throat wide open. Hagan dragged the body into a drain cut. Stripped the big lad bare, and pilfered coin and purse. He didn't need the cudgel, but stowed the three throwing knives up his sleeve.

Dirty shirt three sizes too big for him. Hagan was tall but lean as a whip, there'd be more flesh on a sparrow these days. He found some jerky in the man's pocket and stuffed the contents into his mouth. He was thirsty. Time for a tavern as he dared not test the water in this city. Stale water meant slow death.

He walked on, back straighter, face knife-sharp, eyes scanning streets, alleys, walking up, closer and thicker into the city main. Less crap here, the streets were widening to avenues and he needed to be careful. Not so many scumbags here, Hagan would stick out like a swollen thumb.

But he needed a drink and somewhere to glean information. Fortunately, opportunity provided. *Serendipity—sometimes you have to help it along.* A wealthy looking fellow took a wrong turn. Red cloak, expensive boots, the fool stopped to take a leak in a side cut. Hagan detoured craftily. Crept up behind the man. Poor fellow was drunk, and fiddling with his drawstrings. He grunted as Hagan's knife hilt cracked open the back of his skull.

This lad was more his size, though a bit shorter. It would suffice. Hagan stripped, and redressed in the unconscious man's clean garb. It smelled perfumed which had his nose crinkling, so used to smelling shit.

Thanks, mate.

Hagan stepped out into the alley a different person. Cloaked, booted; the fit was perfect. *Made for me.* He wore a hat that covered his head and allowed him to mask his features. Two more knives and a second sword. This curved towards the point and hardly used.

Better still, a purse containing three gold coins and a jingle of silver.

Tavern time…

Hagan walked briskly now, more confident — another well-heeled visitor to the city. He looked the part as long as no one smelled him. That would be bad. He needed a wash, but first had to drink plenty lest he weaken further.

A tavern. Shabby broken door hanging on one hinge. Hagan shoved it aside and wandered in. A girl squinted at him with her one good eye.

"We're closed—so fuck off."

"Thanks," Hagan said and took seat on the battered stool, facing the taproom. "But I think you can help me."

"Orn!" The woman yelled to someone upstairs and Hagan heard heavy feet approaching from a back door. "You were warned," the woman said. "Now my bro's going to bust your skull open."

Orn was a brute, even bigger than the alley thug Hagan had murdered this morning. He grabbed a cudgel from behind the counter and swung hard at Hagan's face.

Bad idea. And just the encouragement Hagan needed. He caught the club mid-swing and pulled Orn close, upsetting his balance so the big lad almost fell on him. Hagan butted him hard, knocking his head back, and then chewed at Orn's nose until he cried out in alarm.

The woman heaved a chair and circled on him screeching like an abandoned kettle. Hagan knocked her off her feet and slipped a stolen knife into his hand. He pricked Orn beneath his jaw, a small bead of blood getting the thug's attention.

"I need water, clean water. Your bitch sister can fetch it." Orn nodded, and the woman staggered to her feet, swore at him, but returned with a pitcher she slammed on the counter, its frothy contents spilling over.

Hagan switched hands, keeping his left on the blade. He swiveled on the stool and pored the cool liquid into his mouth, spilling half of it on his lap. Didn't matter, he soon felt better.

"I need information," Hagan smiled at the woman.

"We don't know nothing,"

"Well, then I'll just cut his throat open, and while he's dying pass the time by giving you a good stoking. That done, I'll gut you too," *The way you deal with these sort of people. Crude but effective.* It worked. She looked scared for the first time, and Orn made a gurgling noise.

"Glad you appreciate the situation," Hagan smiled, pricking Orn's throat again. "There are northerners in this city. Mercenaries. Where do I find them?"

"Don't know," the woman said, and Hagan pricked Orn again.

"Try harder."

"He knows," she motioned her brother.

"Well played," Hagan grinned, and lightning fast switched the knife point to rest under Orn's left eyeball. "But you see I've a trust issue with you pair. So Orn can speak or lose an eye."

"The *Green Duck* on Upper Dock Street. Close by the tanneries," Orn spat the words out, his sweat dripping on the floor. "It's not far, close to the west gates leading to the upper city. Less than a mile. Keep climbing, the lanes will lead you there."

"Thank you," Hagan said pleasantly. "I've enjoyed this little visit. If you've lied I'll return and kill you both, and torch this shithole to cinders." He stood, slammed the knife hilt into Orn's temple and pushed him forward. The woman yelled, but Hagan kicked her to the floor and left without further ado.

He'd had water, food, and now he had a plan. Life was looking up.

***

Borgil hated Permio as much as his mates. But whereas they spent most their waking hours bitching about it, he took a more practical view. A man could get rich here. Bide your time, do a few local jobs. Killing, robbing for the right people. Stay clear of the Elite like most sensible folk. Big city, plenty of room for everyone.

Outlawed in the north, Borgil and his team had ridden down here with the High King's posse hard up their arses. They'd reached Raleen and laid low for a time. But that country, although fiercely independent, was still part of the Four Kingdoms—and the High King's arm reached down there too.

Permio was their salvation. Last stop before the hangman's noose. Surrounded by desert on three sides, and sea to the north, the Narion's Delta coiling around the Upper City like a fat lazy snake. Be hard to invade a place like this. But easy to make a living for those who kept their heads screwed on.

Borgil determined to do that. Fond of his head, he always wore his kettle helm despite the wretched heat. It was his trademark, that and the queer eating habits. *Badger Borgil* the lads called him on account of his taste for road kill. *You take what's on offer in this life. Don't pay to be fussy.*

Besides, he liked the *Green Duck.* An odd name for a tavern. Borgil hadn't seen any ducks in the vicinity. *Perhaps on the river?* The hostelry was well run and the grog not half bad. The lasses were easy, but you had to be careful lest you catch something. Coffee was good too, and the odd smoke.

And they liked northerners, or at least pretended to. Borgil's boys had straightened out some of the local gangs, putting a halt to the protection racket in this corner of the city.

They'd only been here three months, arriving at the end of the war between the sultan in Sedinadola and the rebels from the trading city Agmandeur—wild deranged tribesmen led by some savage they called Wolf of the Desert. Borgil had never been to the desert and had no desire to go. Flies and dust and bugger all else. Why go there?

They had everything they needed in Cappel Cormac.

The *Duck* was busy this morning, the girls weaving back and forth with dishes and mugs. Borgil reached across and squeezed one's behind. She winked at him and faded off into the kitchens. Borgil would catch up with that one later.

Lazy morning. The lads were dicing, save Coly and Dol who were away down the docks checking on vessels, and newcomers in town. Borgil's team were unofficially working for the big man away in Sedinadola. Of course, no one ever mentioned that, and the Crimson Elite would ignore that small detail were an altercation to occur.

That said, it kept the common rogues at bay. They'd cleaned up this part of town. Twelve big northern lads. Veterans of the eastern frontier where the Four Kingdoms held back the barbarians who continued to raid out of the endless forests of Leeth. Some were retired Bears, others deserters. Redhead Dol was an ex-Tiger who'd been thrown out the regiment for murdering a corporal. Good lad, Dol. Nasty temper.

Borgil was originally from Kella City but the three regiments had turned him down—even the Wolves, who weren't normally that fussy. That was part of the reason he took to robbing the Great South Way. Made a good income until Lord Caswallon, the High King's new enforcer, took an interest and sent a squad of thugs to nail him.

Borgil had bolted to Kelthara the outlaw city—Caswallon's claws had small influence there. He'd met the others, decided on this long-term career plan. Tenacious Caswallon wouldn't stop until they were swinging.

So here they were in this filthy stinking fleshpot. Dicing, drinking, screwing and fighting like pike circling in a muddy lake.

The door creaked open spilling sunlight into the taproom. One of the lads swore, Borgil turned and saw a man standing there. A silhouette framed by glare, tall, lean, two swords hanging from a belt.

Borgil reached for his ax and rose slowly from his stool. Strangers were enemies in this place.

He approached the door, two of the others joining him. The man said nothing, stood there gazing at them. He took a step forward. Borgil took stock. Lanky, confident, stank of shit but was garbed well enough. A thief, obviously. Murderer, most likely. Borgil slapped the ax haft into his left palm and blocked the entrance.

"Don't think I know you," Borgil said.

"Name's Hagan—I'm Morwellan."

"Not your fault," Borgil said. "I've heard they're all goat fuckers up there."

"Sheep," Hagan smiled at him showing perfect white teeth, his eyes gray as winter seas. "The goats are too agile."

"You're in the wrong tavern," Strain the Rope said, standing beside Borgil, a long, wickedly curved knife in his hands, the red scarf hiding the torn tissue on his neck.

"Sign said Green Duck," Hagan said stepping forward and stopping as Borgil and his men checked his progress. "I'm wanting an ale. Be good fellows and step aside."

"Go," Borgil slapped the ax in his palm again. "We don't need Morwellans, especially if they all smell like you."

"Unfortunate happenstance," the man Hagan said. "I was ditched by my companion, left in the shit. You might know him. Operates down here. Tall fellow, scar on forehead. Fucking great sword."

"That's got to be Corin an Fol," Rejen said joining them from a corner. Rej had his blade drawn and was pointing it at the newcomer. "He's not welcome here either."

"Well then you can help me find him so I can shove a sword up his arse," Hagan said, taking another step into the taproom.

"You're a confident bastard," Borgil said. "There are ten of us in here, legal employees of the sultan. Charged with cleaning up this quarter. That means eradicating shitheads like you, and Corin an Fol—whoever the fuck he is?" Borgil shot a questioning glance to Rejen who shrugged.

"Got a reputation, heard him mentioned once or twice. A renegade Wolf. Down here during the war. Survived a massacre in the desert—only one as did. Last I knew he'd gone back north."

"I was with him last week," Hagan said folding his arms. He looked bored, and Borgil was almost impressed by the man's arrogance. How this Hagan had survived in Cappel with an attitude like that was remarkable. "I'd like to catch up with him again," Hagan said.

Borgil saw movement to his left—his girl was back lingering in the corner. Time to deal with this pest. "You need to leave, Morwellan, else I cut a few chunks off your skinny hide."

"You can try," Hagan smiled, the fingers of his right hand brushing the sword on that side. The left hand held a knife. *Where the fuck had that come from?*

Borgil stepped forward. Swung hard and fast…

***

And Hagan leaped aside, his tossed knife pinned the rangy one with the scarf's arm to the doorframe, and his right boot impacted the brute with the kettle helm. He stepped forward, rammed his sword pommel up under the big man's chin. Kettle head slumped to the rushes.

The third man swung across with his broadsword but the blade stuck in the door, Hagan winked at him and then kicked him hard in the balls.

The remaining seven were on their feet, dice discarded and faces red with rage. The girls and odd customer looked on with interest, things not going as they'd expected.

The seven surrounded him, blades leveled. Hagan stepped over Kettle Helm and stowed his knife. "I was just playing," he said, hinting their three friends on the floor. "If you boys want to increase the stakes, then do step forward." They blinked, the sun's glare in their faces, and eyes widened seeing the second sword appear in Hagan's other hand.

"You scraggy cats are no match for me," Hagan said, stepping forward and smiling as the seven backed away. "Be sensible. All I'm after is a drink and friendly chat."

"We'll kill you," one said.

"I expect so," Hagan smiled at that one. "But, you know—I don't much fucking care. Been a shit year, and a man has to die sometime. Why not today? Besides, I'll take half of you wankers with me." He smiled again.

"He's a fucking nutter," another one said. But they hadn't moved, seemed uncertain what to do. On the floor Kettle Helm groaned and rose to his knees. Hagan booted him in the face and he slumped forward again.

"Make your mind up time," Hagan let the blades dance in his hands. "I'm having that beer, lads."

The nearest shrugged and stowed his blade, a long-haired rogue with pony tail and eye-patch. "Let him through," he said. "Every man deserves a drink before they die."

"Sensible fellow," Hagan glided through to the counter as the men surrounded him again. "Large one," Hagan said to the nearest girl. "You boys can relax." he rested the swords against the counter.

"Enjoy your drink," Eye-patch said. "You're leaving here in a box. They stood over him as the girl poured a tankard full of honey colored ale. Hagan downed the contents and belched.

"Ah, that's better. Got my second wind." He stood slowly, wiped his mouth, half turned, and snapped a palm lightning-fast into Eye-patch's face. That one fell away but the other six were on him.

Hagan tossed a stool at one, taking him in the knees. He dived and rolled, hurled a knife at the next man pinning his wrist to the wall, kicked number three in the face, then jumped sideways and elbowed the next one trying to cut his throat from behind. Hagan stamped on that fellow's foot and grabbed his balls with a hand, slamming up against the wall, the back of his head ramming, impacting a nose. He vaulted over to where the swords rested, retrieved the blades and swung them in unison.

The two left standing watched those swords for a moment and decided to call it a day. Kettle Helm was on his feet again, but looked a bit sick.

"What did you say your name was?" Kettle asked.

"Hagan, formerly of House Delmorier. Now an outlaw and renegade due to unfair circumstances."

"Welcome to the *Duck*," Kettle Helm rose to his feet and yelled the girls get ale for all. "I'm Borgil, and these are my crew. Think you'll fit well enough in our gang. You seem to have the right attitude."

"I'm not joining," Hagan said. "I'm leading. You boys are looking at your new boss." Strangely no one contradicted him.

Later that day, hard into his cups, Hagan questioned Borgil about the situation in Cappel Cormac—explaining how he'd only just arrived and had fallen foul of the Crimson Elite already. Thanks to that longshanks with the big sword.

"Elite are vicious," Borgil said. "The sultan loves them nearly as much as his administrators, tax collectors, and priests. And they don't like us— the Crimson— though we're tolerated as we clean up their messes. Twats are overrated," Borgil said and Hagan assumed this was a bone of contention.

"What about this Corin an Fol?" Hagan asked Eye-patch, whose name he'd learned was Dilan.

"Know him by reputation only," Dilan said. "Something of a legend in the city. We arrived after he'd left. Think he was thrown out the Wolves."

"People don't get thrown out of the Wolves," Borgil laughed. "They get thrown in."

"It's what I heard," Dilan said. "He doesn't like us Bears much, but I can't say I blame him for that. General Belmarius tossed me and Ropey Strain over there out of the regiment for pilfering. Strain took it hard, killed a few lads at scoff. Belmarius let him swing for a time. Luckily, I found him, and cut the noose. Strain don't say much on account of his squeaky voice. I heard they rejected you," this last comment to Borgil who scowled.

"Fuck the Bears, I say," Borgil said. "We're free men down here."

"So where is Corin now?" Hagan asked but no one knew and he was content to let the matter rest, especially as one of the girls had come and sat on his knee, her nimble fingers unlacing his drawstrings and fumbling beneath.

"Think I'll call it a day." Hagan allowed the girl to lead him upstairs. He saw them watching him leave. He'd sleep with a knife in each hand tonight. But first there was another appetite to appease.

Chapter 5 | Too Late

"So, what's your plan—bitch?" The slap sent her sprawling, and the kick hurt so bad she started sobbing again. "Father's going to find you and cut you open."

Nalissa crumpled to a kneel, and wrapped her bruised arms around her knees, the fresh tears mingling with old stains. She knew she was a mess, lip badly swollen, hair disheveled, clothes torn and stained by grime. Her captor looked at her with cool dispassion, like a fisher observing the day's catch.

She stood legs braced—the ship's tossing below her feet, wind billowing her hair and triangular sails above. Motionless in the motion, feet braced. Cat lithe—a killer, confident, arrogant, and calm. Then she smiled. Nalissa feared her most at times like this.

"You're just a spoilt little girl," the woman said. "You know nothing of this world."

"I've done nothing to you—don't deserve…this." Nalissa wiped the tears from her cheek. She hated showing weakness to her captor. The woman had stitched her lip the other night down in woods by the tiny campfire she'd built. As the needle and thread were ruthlessly applied, Nalissa had held back the tears. That sharp pain was a small thing compared to what waited ahead.

"Deserve?" The woman laughed. "Poor child, few of us get what we deserve. Anyway, It's not personal—just business. It's how I make my living."

"Torturing women."

"Sometimes." That quirky grin again. "Whatever the customer wants."

"What will happen to me?"

"I'm selling you, my dear," that smile again. "For a fat profit. My...client... wants to hurt your father. His is a more personal grievance, I'm thinking. Clearly the merchant has a soft spot for his only daughter. From the state of you, that's obvious. And you were a very easy target. I've already been paid good coin, and get to keep the proceeds from the sale. Win-win for me. But I need you looking your best when we reach Permio."

"You're not taking me to Permio—you won't get past Port Sarfe," Nalissa said. "Whoever you're working for doesn't know my father. They—and you—have made a bad mistake."

"We'll see." The woman looked out at the water; there were dolphins out there. The rain had stopped and a thin strip of sunlight gilded the horizon. Nalissa studied her enemy. That unusual pale face, the long shiny black hair, flowing free this morning but normally tied back in pigtail. The confident, disdainful poise, and that terrifying smile.

"I'll stab you when you're not looking."

"Thanks for keeping me informed," the woman laughed. "Not very bright—are you."

They'd boarded at first light after the five-day ride. The woman—Nalissa still didn't know her name had paid some coin to the captain of a large merchantman. Enough coin to seal his lips, though the man didn't look happy, and he'd avoided any eye contact with Nalissa—the snake.

The crew kept their distance. They were uncomfortable around women, who were rumored unlucky as cargo. *Superstitious fools.* But it was more than that. Her captor scared them shitless, Nalissa had seen how they always hurried to avoid her.

"Time for you to get some beauty rest," the woman turned and gazed down at her again. "We're sharing a cabin—the captain's own. I like my comfort, so I'm taking his bed. You're sleeping on the floor." She reached down and grabbed Nalissa's hair, yanking her to her feet. Then she pushed her forward towards the hatch leading below.

Nalissa saw two sailors watching, their faces embarrassed, ashamed. *So you should be, you bastards.* Nalissa spat at the nearest as she clambered through the hatch, the door clamping down behind her.

***

"You've just missed it," the harbor master told him as Corin paced, tom-cat jumpy on the jetty. "Last merchantman left an hour ago."

Fuck.

"Were there two women on board?" Corin had to restrain himself from grabbing the man's throat. Not his fault. *But I'd really like to hit someone.* He'd condensed a five-day ride into three, nearly killed two horses and himself riding break-neck through woods and valleys, cutting across country. Eventually crashing upon Kador Harbor. "I asked whether there were women?"

The harbormaster shrugged. "Don't know," he said "I was having a smoke in the office when it left. Captain Shomer don't usually haul lasses. Crew get boisterous with them onboard."

"These are not average lasses," Corin decided he might hit the harbormaster anyway.

"I saw them," a young docker called across from another jetty.

Obviously, he'd been eavesdropping. Corin left the harbormaster and sprinted over to grab the young lad by his scruff.

"You sure?"

"Certain," the lad looked grumpy. "Get off me!"

Corin let him go. "Cause if you're pissing in my pot I'll shove this where the sun doesn't shine." He tapped Clouter's pommel with a knuckle. The lad blinked.

"That's a big sword."

"Yes, and I know how to use it," Corin said. "Now listen. Tell me what you saw, who they were. What they looked like, behaved. Everything. I'm tired, hungry and very pissed off—so I suggest you start right away."

"She said they were sisters," the lad told him after recounting what he saw at sun up. "The pale one had the other in her arms. Said she was sick. She didn't look sick, but mad as a nest of hornets. I caught her eyes, though her face was buried in a hood. Real pretty."

Good—she's showing some grit.

"Tell me about the pale sister," Corin's mind was racing. They would have to restock at Sarfe. Every ship did. Took on marines, extra weaponry lest the slave galleys strike from Sedinadola. Fishers were usually left alone, but not rich merchantmen. That tub would be calling in at Port Sarfe in a couple of days. He had to get there first.

I need another horse.

"Scary eyes."

"What?" Corin's mind jolted. He'd forgotten where he was for a moment. "Who?"

"The pale one... there was something," he shuffled, looked awkward. "Unnatural about her."

"In what way?"

"Hard to say. She was *very* pale, kind of pretty but her eyes were cruel. Cold as cats'."

"You got that close?"

"I was the one who cast them off. She blew me a kiss—Cats' Eyes did."

"How sweet."

"It wasn't," he said. "Felt more like a threat."

"You obviously mix with the wrong women," Corin said.

"She seemed… half animal. Like a spirit cat—the way she walked, more like a slinky prowl." He stuck a finger in his mouth and wriggled a loose tooth. Corin smiled. *Take your time.* "She was graceful, and knew it. Arrogant. I didn't much like her."

Corin nodded. *A cat woman. That's a novelty, not come across many of those.* "You keep horses here?"

"In town. The City Guard have a score or so at the stables. Don't rent them out, though."

"They will this time," Corin slapped a silver coin in the lad's fist and strode from the jetty.

"Any luck?" the harbormaster shouted out. Corin ignored him.

Kador lay squeezed between two steep hills. A rough trading port at the northwest corner of Raleen. Unlike the rest of the country, Kador was cold and it rained here incessantly. It was drizzling, as Corin wrapped the guardhouse with his knuckles.

"Who's that?" A gruff voice from above his head.

"Name's Corin — I need a horse."

"Bugger off!"

Corin hit the doors this time making them rattle. "I'm not moving until you provide me with a horse," he called up. A face appeared surrounded by a helmet, a second one moments later. Then a different voice spoke from somewhere behind them.

"Go see who that idiot is, then chase him off or drag him inside for a beating."

"We're on it, Captain," helmet and faces vanished. Minutes later, after a lot of clonking and kerfuffle, the doors creaked ajar. The guards stared at Corin. Then they stared at Clouter shoved point-first in the wet mud.

"You'd better come here, Captain," the biggest soldier said. Corin leant on the crosspiece.

It's fine, really. I've got all fucking day.

An angry-faced portly looking soldier with a broad red sash on his tunic muscled out between the guards. He looked tired and disheveled with fresh wine stains on his shirt. He saw the longsword and gulped.

"What can we do for you?"

"I need a horse. Yesterday."

"We don't lend out horses—we're not a fucking charity."

Corin sighed. "You'll be needing charity if you don't get me a nag. A four-legged racing nag, not a donkey. I need to get to Sarfe soonest."

"Now listen—"

Corin stepped forward, swung Clouter full circle and slammed it point down in the mud again, an inch from where it had been before. "I work for Silon the merchant. You might have heard of him. He's a bit upset at the moment, which means I'm upset too. Someone's stolen something very precious from Silon and I need to apprehend the thief and get it back. Understand?"

"Silon's a big cheese, Captain," the smaller guard said.

"I know who he is," the captain squared his shoulders, tried to exude authority, and then looked down noticing his wine stains for the first time. "But Silon has no authority in Kador."

Corin sighed. "Then I'll have to do this the hard way." He hefted Clouter again.

Half hour later Corin was riding the Captain's favorite stallion out the city making for the Port Sarfe highway. It was surprising what a longsword can do to an oak door when wielded with enough incentive. Corin hoped they had good carpenters in Kador. That Captain would have some explaining to do when the City Council convened to discuss the state of the guard house.

Now for another long hard ride, with no food or ale in his belly.

**

Nalissa wiped spew from her mouth and coughed up fresh blood from her lip wound. The woman stood over her again. The pain from that last kick had her doubled up and vomiting, the mess adding to her earlier stains left from the ship's relentless rolling. They'd been on the sea three days and Nalissa had decided to fight back.

That hadn't got her very far. "Where are you taking me?" She got the words out between chokes. She braced for another kick, but looked up and saw the woman gazing down at her, her dark eyes narrowed in scrutiny.

"You've got a lot of spirit for a spoilt little whelp," her captor said. "But I'd rein it in my dear, pride precedes a fall. Challenge me again and I'll slit your throat wide open. I have a temper—do not test it."

"Not very professional," Nalissa said and braced again, but the woman laughed, her moods seemed as mercurial as the ocean beneath them.

"You're a cheeky little mare. Almost I could like you. But you shouldn't try my patience so. Accept your fate, Nalissa. Maybe you'll have a decent master who won't flog you every day if you please him enough."

"I'm not serving anyone!"

"You'll service everyone until some fool buys you. Permians like to sample their goods before purchase, they're not soft like northern folk."

"You're not from Permio," Nalissa's mind was racing. She had to keep her cool. They'd be mooring at Port Sarfe soon. Probably tonight. She'd escape—somehow. Had to.

"I'm from Shen," the woman's dark eyes narrowed slightly as she turned and gazed out the tiny porthole. "I miss it sometimes. The subtlety, the intricacies of the Magister's Manse."

"I don't know where that is."

"Far side of the world," the woman said, her dark eyes flicking like chips of wet coal. She seemed far away for a moment, lost in some distant memory. *Who are you?*

Outside light was fading, the sea taking on more chop. At least the rolling had withdrawn. Nalissa guessed they'd reached shallower waters. Port Sarfe must be near.

Keep you nerve and keep her talking.

"So why are you here?" Nalissa tucked a stray lock behind an ear.

"What?" The woman still seemed distracted, as though thinking of her distant home. "I was betrayed and banished from Shen," she said after a moment's icy silence.

"Why?" Nalissa suspected she already knew the answer.

"I killed the wrong person," the woman smiled at her. "A man of property and importance. He tried to take advantage of me, so I slit his belly open slowly and left him for the dogs. They put a price on my head—which is why I'm here."

"Hurting other women," Nalissa said. Outside her window it was getting dark. They should be docking soon. *Hold on!*

"I told you this isn't personal," the woman said, turning and staring down at her again. "I attended the school of arms at Ta Shen where I learnt my trade as an assassin. I already possessed other skills, so took to the training with ease. Since I can no longer work in my own land I make do here in the west. You were a priority case—I got paid handsomely in advance, which rarely happens."

"By whom?"

"Ha—good try," the woman laughed again. She looked younger when she laughed, and Nalissa tried guessing her age. Perhaps twenty-five, maybe thirty. Hard to tell. That face was so pale, the large dark eyes and long black hair again tied neatly back. The expression alert, in control. "Clients are always confidential. Suffice to say someone who doesn't care for your father."

Nalissa changed tack. "You never told me your name."

"And I never shall," the woman said straightening her back and looking at the porthole again. "Names hold power." After a moment she turned, her expression almost comradely. "They call me the Lynx in Permio."

'When do we dock?" Nalissa said; she couldn't stand it any longer, but the woman just laughed at her and made for the cabin door.

"Get some sleep," the Lynx said. "But first clear up that mess you've made—stinks in here. I'm off for a drink, expect those sailors have grog hidden somewhere."

"I doubt they'll share it with you," Nalissa spat the words out.

"Doubt they'll have much choice," the cabin door slammed shut. Nalissa rolled onto her back and then staggered to her knees. *State of me.* She was aching and bruised, her long legs scratched and bloody, her garments shredded, and her hair matted with blood where the Lynx had ripped a chunk free. At least her lip was numb, the salt air healing the wound and those deftly sewn stiches reduced to an itch. *This will be over soon. The nightmare ended. Hold it together for a few more hours.*

Easy to say. Nalissa threw herself on the creaking cot and wept from sheer frustration. One chance. She had to escape when they were at Port Sarfe. *Why weren't they there yet?* She'd slip ashore— somehow. Run, and scream, anything to draw attention. The Watch would find her, know who she was. Then the Lynx had better watch out for herself.

Nalissa managed a savage smile. Pale-face would be hanging from the gibbet in the city square by breakfast tomorrow.

Chapter 6 | Foiled Again

Corin reined in and leaned forward in his saddle. The horse was on the point of collapse, but the lights below winked up at him. Port Sarfe, scarce ten miles distant. Night falling; he'd arrived in South Raleen three and a half days after galloping down from Kador.

No ship could make that journey inside three full days. Corin grinned and rubbed the horse's neck. "Sorry boy, been a rough trip. But you've done me proud. That tub won't depart till first light, even if it's docked already. I can get you stabled, and me some ale. Hah!" He urged the beast forward at a walk and guided it down the road, winding through sandstone ravines that eventually led down to the city.

Corin reached the *Crooked Knife* just as the Night Watch tolled the hour bell. Quiet in Port Sarfe tonight. He left the horse with Rado's groom and, after downing a quick ale, ventured out to the harbor.

A merchantman. There wouldn't be many this far south as most traders kept to safer waters, and merchants venturing to Permio usually took the road south and concealed their identity. Thus he should have no problem finding the ship and slipping on board.

Corin paced the docks end to end—twice. Port Sarfe was much bigger than Kador, but not large enough to hide a full-size merchantman. *Should be here by now.* Finally, frustrated, and exhausted, Corin stumbled back into the *'Knife* to ask Rado if he'd seen the ship.

But it was Silon the merchant who met Corin at the tavern door.

"So, you failed." Silon stood in the doorway, his expression, bitter, and arms folded in contempt.

"Where's the ship?" Corin said. "Enlighten me, and I'll steal onboard and get her back. Leave it to me."

"You were meant to save her at Atarios," Silon said.

"I tried, but my horse didn't have wings," Corin said. He made to push through to the taproom but Silon blocked his passage. "I tried the docks at Kador too, been bloody everywhere. Just missed them at Kador, so the ship must be docking here—surprised it isn't here yet."

"She's called the Lynx," Silon said, finally letting Corin through, and nodding to Rado to get them both some ale.

"Who?"

"Nalissa's captor, you imbecile. They call her the Lynx." Silon snatched the ale from Rado's fist and downed the contents then wiped froth from his mouth. "I hate fucking beer," he said, slapping the mug back into Rado's hands. The innkeep blinked. "But I'll take a refill."

Rado nodded and departed promptly.

Corin was thinking. *Cat woman. Lynx. Some kind of assassin.* He scratched an ear. "Docker in Kador spotted them boarding. Said the woman was pale and had cruel eyes like a cat."

"Hence the name," Silon said, his lip curling.

"The lad said she scared him," Corin ignored the sarcasm. "Something unnatural about her—he said."

"She's a known killer," Silon's face was grim. "I've done some digging. The Lynx attended the Assassin's Guild in Shen. Was one of their top people until she killed one of the Magister's family and got banished. She disappeared for years and turned up recently. Now works out of Permio mostly."

"Then why haven't I heard of her?"

Silon laughed bitterly. "Most people haven't. The Lynx doesn't like attention. Once you know her name you're next on her death list."

"And now she's working for Caswallon, way up in Kella City, you think?" Corin glugged his ale then stopped when Silon grabbed his arm.

"I need you sober."

"I haven't eaten for two days and I need a drink," Corin said. "Can't think properly without ale." He was exhausted, confused and very hungry. And seeing Silon here had dampened any satisfaction he'd felt in reaching Sarfe in such good time. "Where's the ship?" Corin said.

"Not here," Silon said. Corin just looked at him.

"Permio bound." Silon said, after a moment. "Be mooring at Cappel Cormac in a few days, I'd wager my best earring on it." He waggled the diamond as surety.

"I thought they always stopped at Sarfe?" Corin wiped ale from his mouth. He needed to sit down somewhere before he fell over. *Gods I'm weary.* "Too dangerous entering Permian waters without escort, or soldiers on board."

"So, it is," Silon said. "But doubtless she persuaded the captain to proceed."

"I'm going back to Permio," Corin said as the realization hit him.

"Looks like it," Silon said, awarding Corin an icy smile. "Sit down before you fall down. Eat something, then crash upstairs. I've had Rado prepare you a room. I'll expect you on the road before dawn."

"You…*knew* I was coming?" Corin struggled to keep his thoughts in a row.

"Since you left a trail of lame horses and broken guard rooms—yes," Silon barked a laugh. "Pigeons fly. I make it my business to stay informed, Corin an Fol."

Rado brought some fish and potatoes and Corin took to a corner table shoving the piping contents into his mouth. Silon joined him but refused a plate of food. "I've scant appetite," the merchant said.

"I'll have his," Corin told Rado but the innkeep was away serving others, the inn having got busy as the late evening rush took hold.

"Feel better?" Silon was watching Corin as he dapped bread into the source covering his fish. He didn't respond until he'd mopped up everything on the plate.

"Much better."

"Good," Silon said. "I need you at your best, mercenary. Get her back in good health and spirit and you'll be rewarded, handsomely. I assure you. Fail, and you're out of a fucking job. Understand?"

"Understood."

Silon stood up and made to depart. "The Lynx will take her to Sedinadola."

"That's the Sultan's Royal City," Corin was horrified. Bad enough returning to Cappel Cormac. Entering Sedinadola was suicidal for a northerner. Since the war the sultan had banned any armed soldiers in that city saving his elite Crimson Guard. To be seen with a sword was to be disemboweled in the Royal Piazza at high noon.

"The denizens of the Royal City pay well for slaves." Silon almost spat the last word out. "Caswallon wants to rip chunks off me piece by piece."

"I can't go near Sedinadola with Clouter. It'd be like waving a bloody flag," Corin said. "And I'll need help."

"You'll have to get a team together in Cappel," Silon said. "A crack force, with some trustworthy natives who can report on the slave markets in Sed."

"Trustworthy?" Corin spat a fish bone onto his plate. "We're talking about Permio, I—"

"—Will work it out," Silon said. "There must be northerners in Cappel you know, or know of. They will help for enough coin. And I have lots of coin, Corin an Fol. Do not report back without my daughter." The merchant turned and brusquely made for the door, the inn's occupants parting to let him through.

Fuck it.

Corin sipped his third ale, the inn dark and silent surrounding him. An hour passed, two. *Getting late.* He should have turned in, but had to think things through. *Back to Permio—already.* The dust wouldn't have settled in Cappel Cormac since his last visit, so he'd need extra discretion. Not one of his skills. Corin was more of a bust in and get the work done type. Hated creeping about in the dark.

He stopped mid sup, spotting Rado over by the door bidding a customer good night. *Where's that girl?* Corin sat bolt upright as a memory flashed through. There was something he needed to ask the innkeep right away.

"Rado."

"What?" The patron glanced his way and continued his conversation with the sailor at the door. "Get Tashi," Corin yelled, making several people jump at a table close by. They stared angrily at him.

"Sorry," Corin said. They turned away and recommenced their conversations. Occasionally one would glance his way and scowl. Corin forgot about them as Rado wiped his apron and approached Corin's ale-stained table.

"What's the problem?" Rado was ready to close shop, and clearly in no mood for Corin's witticisms.

"I need see to see that girl—Tashi."

"So, do I," Rado wiped sweat from his face. "Sly bitch disappeared with the entire months takings morning after you left."

"She did what?" Corin stood up spilling ale and receiving more hostile glances from the party in the corner.

"Yes," Rado said, and that explained his sad expression this evening. "I'm out of pocket, Corin—and short-staffed to boot."

But Corin wasn't listening. He was picturing a pale face and a smugly amused grin. Tashi. *But that's impossible — she'd have to have flown to Atarios to get there before me.* "It's just a coincidence," he muttered to himself remembering how the words she'd said were the same as those carved on the wall outside Nalissa's room. "Gods I need sleep."

"A bloody thief," Rado said, thinking Corin was addressing him. "I'll whip the lean bitch dry if I see her again."

"She's long gone," Corin said, and then added, "I imagine," hurriedly, after catching Rado's quizzical eye. "You said she hadn't worked for you long."

"Long enough to know where I kept the proceeds," Rado slunk into a chair beside Corin. "I'm too old for this bollocks."

But Corin was too worried about the next few days to give any thought to Rado's woes. "You said she was bright?"

"Sharp, yes. But what's it to you? Tashi's gone. History."

Corin nodded. *Just coincidence and my tired mind.* "I'm sure you're right," he said. "And sorry you're skint. But if I don't hit the sack in the next ten minutes I'm sleeping here." Corin left Rado to his moping, and made for the door. "Night, night," he said to the moody party clustered around the table in the corner, playing cards.

"Who is that dotard?" Corin heard one of them grumble.

"They call him the Gray Wolf," someone else added. "Don't upset him."

"Works for Silon," replied yet another and a series of muttering followed. Corin made the stairs, hauled his long frame up and kicked open the spare bedroom door. He fell on the bed and was snoring inside a minute.

Chapter 7 | The Secret

The world was black outside their cabin. There was a constant rolling motion and sounds of timbers creaking, wind whistling through cracks, surge of ocean below. Aside from that, nothing. No calls from sailors announcing land, no heave of anchor, or plaintive cry of shorebirds. Occasionally a wash of seawater would smack against the porthole glass. Nalissa had wept herself dry. Only hatred stopped the flow. They'd avoided Port Sarfe. That news had almost broken her. *Almost.*

The sickly smile on the Lynx's face when she told her was the one thing that had saved Nalissa. *I'm going to stick a knife in that smile. Dig out those molars, those perfect teeth, one by one. You won't be smiling then, bitch.*

Anger. *Rage* — the only weapon she had. Better than despair. To despair was to perish. *I'm Silon's daughter.* Her father would find and save her. Or more likely the man that worked for her father.

Corin.

She pictured the ungainly mercenary's craggy face that night when they'd made love in her father's gardens. A pure whim on her part, Corin was so refreshingly different from the noblemen and wealthy sons of merchants and towns people she knew back in Atarios.

Wild and unruly, with the manners of a goat. How he had excited her that night, stomping and crashing about. Subtle as a bull in a market stall. But the only man brave enough—or stupid enough—to go after her.

But what could Corin or her father do? The Lynx had told her their destination. Sedinadola—The sultan's city. As hostile a place as could be imagined. The Permians were rumored to be as cruel as pestilence. They would break her spirit down there. Destroy her. That was what the Lynx said, the cat-cream smile creeping from her lips.

I will survive. You're not winning this. Nalissa knew she was fooling herself. It was all she could do to hide her tears when the Lynx returned, her breath stinking of brandy, and a whip in her hands.

"Strip," the Lynx said, her dark eyes huge and dilated.

Nalissa did as she was told and sat naked on the bed. "You won't get a good price if I'm ripped bloody," she said watching as the woman stooped over her, prodding here and there, resting the whip against her flesh so she almost jumped in horror.

"We could be lovers," the Lynx kneeled beside her and kissed Nalissa's cheek so very softly. "Make the voyage more enjoyable," she nibbled an ear, cupped a breast with her hand, and then stood up quickly and lashed out with the whip, catching Nalissa across the thigh.

She yelped, then the tears came again. The Lynx stared at her for a moment and then tossed the whip on the floor by the bed. Nalissa glared at it as though it were a serpent ready to strike.

"We'll port in Syrannos in five days," the Lynx said. "The crew are eager to reach their destination after our last…discussion."

"I thought we we're making to the Royal City?"

"Plans change," the Lynx said. "You should get some sun tomorrow. You're looking weak as a lily, my dear."

Above deck the captain stood alongside his pilot, the waves crashing below their feet as the ship tossed and cut through waves. They'd changed course. The captain hadn't wanted too but it was hard to argue with razor steel probing beneath your eyelid.

"We're not stopping at Port Sarfe." The woman had found him in his cabin. Crept in and helped herself to his brandy. He'd thrown a punch. Bad mistake, she'd hissed, kicked out at his knee knocking him off balance and then stuck that knife under his eye.

"Syrannos." He'd nodded enthusiastically and informed his men at once. No mutiny; his boys knew the risk but there was something terrifying about the pale woman. And where was her companion? Sick in that cabin, not eating or drinking. No one had seen her since earlier today.

"We'll get rid of them and make for Cappel," the captain told his companion. The grizzle-faced pilot didn't look happy.

"That's if those galleys don't spot us first, Captain." They both knew the hazards of approaching Permio without escort or marines on board to stave off attack. Permian Slavers were shallow drafted; they kept to the coastline, travelling west and south to far-off lands like Golt and Yamondo. But approaching Syrannos would be touch and go. And there were Crenise pirates in these waters too.

"Well, we'll have to stay alert," the captain snapped at his man. Then his jaw dropped seeing a shadow slipping down the port side of the vessel. He nudged the pilot, who jumped in alarm.

"Shush," the captain nudged him. "What's she up to?" The pale-skinned woman and was making for the aft deck. Watching her made the captain think of a tiger he'd seen in Golt, caught by hunters, pacing around and around.

Both men gasped when she vaulted onto the stern rail, her arms stretched wide. What the captain saw next left him speechless and would give him nightmares all week. The woman morphed into a bird—a swan, white as fresh falling snow. Those wings lifted; the long neck stretched forward, and she was gone. Out into the night, a glimmer of white and then nothing.

"I need a drink," the pilot said.

***

So good to fly again! She rose up through the night then swooped low and glided level just above the water, stretching out her wings on either side, the feathers glinting in the moonlight. She laughed—a bird cry—feeling the kiss of brine as her wings touched water. *Freedom.* This was how she kept herself young.

The swan/woman flew for hours eventually reaching that distant jungle headland where she alighted softly, and shifted her form a second time. Now she was a cat. Her favorite guise. A lynx, gray and lean. Stealth and claw. Silent hunter. She paced out into the night, stalking. Killing. Hunting again, the jungle closing around her, and everywhere the cries of creatures large and small.

At last satisfied with her night's recreation the Lynx returned to the ocean, became a tern, and for a second time leaped into the night sky. A silent silver arrow, arcing high, winging fast over western ocean. Morning found her settling on the bow of the merchantman.

The tern shrieked, the wings faded and her bird form shifted back to a slim woman clad in black leather trousers, jerkin and knee length boots, her face pale as snowfall. She stole below decks, smiling as she noted the lone watchman's terrified stare.

Her quarry was sleeping, sprawled naked on the bed. That sleek brown skin soaked in sweat. The woman studied that warm flesh: the firm breasts, long muscular legs, moist dark patch between, that cascade of wild smoky hair.

You are a beauty...

The Lynx knelt on the bed and whispered in Nalissa's ear.

"I'll tell you a secret. My name was Ta-Kai back in Shen," she whispered to the sleeping girl. "It means Queen of Cats, my shadow kin. My people the Aikashi are an ancient race who were almost eradicated by you humans. To survive we needed cunning. If you ever hear my name spoken, or utter it yourself you will die." She smiled. Kissed Nalissa's cheek softly as though they were lovers, and curled up content beside her.

"One day I might tell you my story," Ta-Kai breathed softly in the younger woman's ear. Then she closed her eyes and let sleep claim her for one dream free peaceful hour until the morning sun gilded their cabin's porthole and the tanned girl beside her stirred. Ta-Kai seldom slept for long lest the shadow stalkers steal her dreams. Her kin back in Shen – the silent hunters. The only ones she feared.

Chapter 8 | Allies

Corin watched from the prow as a line of palms fanned over sand, and beyond them, brush and scrubby thorns opening on a wide white coastline, dunes parading off into hazy distance.

The Silver Strand. A wide compact beach that linked the Permian cities of Cappel Cormac and Syrannos in the east to the Royal City, Sedinadola. No need for a road, the beach was comprised of tiny broken shells crunched down to dust by countless years of wave and tide.

It was as good to place to land as any in this gods' forsaken country. He'd boarded a shrimp boat and left Port Sarfe at first light, arriving down here yesterday. The shrimper had a seasonal contract with the harbormaster at Syrannos, and was allowed anchorage in that city for an extortionate fee. A charge that Silon always paid, using the shrimper as another clandestine way of accessing this hostile country. Corin had stayed onboard until dark, then slipped into the harbor and pilfered a ketch.

He didn't bother with a sail initially. Just rowed cheerfully out the harbor as though he owned it. Another night fisherman setting out for shrimps and crab. Once clear of the harbor, Corin set the small triangular sail and messed with the tiller, until he trapped enough wind to aim his craft east running parallel with the coastline, until dawn's pale glimmer allowed good view of the open beach.

Corin beached the craft and left it behind, stealing through the palms, the pink light of morning filtering down through those fronds. Clouter was strapped in harness across his back, the long knife at his side, and he carried a small crossbow he'd borrowed from Silon's secret cache at Port Sarfe.

Corin was a crap archer—but if you were close enough you sometimes got lucky. He trotted out onto the white crunchy sand. *The Silver Strand* gleamed for miles in either direction, a hundred yards across from shoreline to scrubby dunes at the southern end.

Glancing back, Corin could just make out the distant spires of Syrannos, a city he'd never had the pleasure to frequent. Ahead lay Cappel Cormac—his destination, and a place he knew only too well. He wasn't happy about returning. Didn't have much of a plan. But he needed help and the only place he'd find that was Cappel.

He walked for over a mile before seeing the first camel station. There were three of the strange humped beasts standing under the canopy of a tent. Corin didn't like camels— bad tempered as the people who ride them. He saw two men seated by a pool, both smoking their curly pipes.

Corin ambled up, smiling. "Good morning," he called across.

The men leaped to their feet, alarmed at seeing a stranger emerge from the palms beside the road. They reached for their scimitars, but Corin was quicker.

He reversed his knife, tossed it deftly at the nearest fellow, the hilt crunching into his skull, then Corin shoulder-charged his companion knocking him off his feet. He butted this one twice in the face with his forehead, breaking the man's nose, then went over to the camels. Freed two, kept the third. The thing spat at him so Corin spat back.

Love you too.

"Just business," Corin told the groaning one with the broken nose.

"I'll need your gear, friend." He hinted and the man stood shakily and slipped off his robe and untied his headdress. Corin glanced over at the other one. Sparked out flat, not going anywhere soon.

Broken Nose glared at him and Corin patted him on the back. "Name's Hagan," he told the man. "I'm from Syrannos." He reached over and lifted the man's curly pipe, took a long pull until his head felt woozy.

"Strange habit," Corin told the man. "I'll stick to my ale. Enjoy your day." Corin clambered into the robe, and wrapped the shemagh around his face with practiced efficiency. *Now the tricky bit.* Corin leaped onto the camel's back and whipped it with a stick he'd found beneath the canvas by their camp. The thing looked at him and started capering about until Corin got it under control.

Twenty minutes later he had the camel pointing in the right direction and started shouting at it, pick up pace along the strand.

By mid-morning Corin spied the round domes and minarets of Cappel Cormac's wealthy sector. He'd avoid that, enter the far gates that opened on the slums by the Narion delta—the tradesmen's entrance to the city. The way he'd slipped in unannounced so many times during the war with Barakani's rebels.

Corin left *The Silver Strand* behind, took the dirt road that skirted the walls. Guards watching from above would see a common trader, merchant, or vagabond making for the poorer sections and docks. Nothing remarkable about that.

The gates by the Narion were open and filled with shabby stinking characters all wedging through the gap, the city markets teeming beyond.

Corin mixed with the crowd, found the closest market and traded his stolen camel for some soup and a fresh loaf. He'd got done over by the evil-eyed trader but that didn't matter. *You have to be pragmatic in this life.*

Corin found a bench in the corner of the market, fruit flies his only companions. *Time to think. Covert and careful.* The robe almost concealed Clouter, although the hilt and pommel poked up above his head. Not ideal, but it would have to do. An extra shoulder blade—hopefully they'd think him deformed and leave him be.

Time to get cracking. Find some lads. Leave this fleshpot, and make for Sedinadola. Once there, set up camp and do some reconnaissance. *Easy.* Corin almost laughed at his predicament, and not for the first time wished he was back in the Wolf Regiment with men who'd watch his back.

Where to find help? He dared not return to any of Silon's safe houses. Caswallon, or whomever was after the merchant, would have had locals keep watch on those fine hostelries. And he'd be mad returning to the *Crimson Moon* anytime soon. Rezala would have the Elite after him in minutes if he showed up there. But there was one establishment he knew in part side of town with just the right kind of clientele.

***

Borgil was bored. There was only so much whoring and drinking a man could do in a month. Besides, it wasn't relaxing here. You daren't nod off lest someone stick a knife in your belly—most likely one of those whores he'd been tupping. Remarkable that he hadn't caught anything yet.

"We need a project," Borgil said to lanky Strain the Rope who was seated with a plump lass on his knee, running greasy fingers through her hair. She looked miserable, but then Strain wasn't easy company. "Some action," Borgil barked in Strain's ear.

Pony-tail Dilan heard him and wandered over. "You bored too?" he said, the chicken thigh protruding from his mouth.

"Shitless," Borgil said. "And where is our illustrious new leader?"

Borgil had had time to think about Hagan's sudden rise of fortune. And when he'd thought about it enough he'd decided he wasn't overly happy. That Morwellan had played them for fools.

"Got any ideas, Rej?" Dilan said, addressing the balding older man leaning across the taproom counter to get a better look at the servant girl's behind. Rejen was good with a blade. Originally from Kelwyn, he'd been banished for raping a farmer's wife. Killed the farmer too, they said. Randy Rej, the boys called him. "You listening?" Dilan said.

"I'm happy enough here," Rejen said, eyes still on the girl. "Why look for trouble when it's sure to find us?"

"Unless there's gold involved."

Gold? Borgil turned and saw a stranger standing at the door way, a huge sword strapped across his back. "Who are you?"

"Name's Corin an Fol," the stranger said unharnessing his longsword and placing it in front of him, his hands resting on the crosspiece. I've some work should you want it?"

Corin an Fol. The legendary Longswordsman who'd earned such a reputation down here during the war. Hagan's new best friend. *Interesting.* Borgil was wondering where the Morwellan had got to when he saw Hagan appeared in the alley outside. Creeping up behind their new arrival.

"You mentioned gold?" Borgil said.

"Lots," Longsword winked at him. Borgil didn't like people winking at him.

"Where?"

"You'll have to earn it." It would have been nice to hear how, but Hagan's pommel impacted Corin an Fol's head from behind and sent him sprawling.

"That was a bit hasty, Captain," Curly Coly said, back from his scouting down by the quay. "If you don't mind my saying so." Hagan ignored him and stepped over the unconscious body.

"Drag that inside," Hagan said, and the fair-haired rangy Coly and stocky Rejen each grabbed one of Corin's arms and hauled him over to the taproom. Corin's head was soaked with blood and Borgil worried that he was dead.

"He mentioned gold before you whacked him," Borgil said. "You should have held back until we heard the bugger speak."

"Call it a personal grudge," Hagan lifted Corin's longsword, unslung it from the scabbard and unclasped the baldric. Hagan swung the sword in an arc—taking out one of the rush lights, a set of drapes and narrowly missing Rejen's ear. "Fuck, this thing's unwieldy," Hagan laughed and dropped the weapon clanging to the floor.

"What about the gold?" Borgil insisted.

"Shut up about the fucking gold," Hagan said. "He'll tell us when he wakes."

"What if he doesn't wake up?" Dilan cut in.

"He will, I put a dent in him not a hole," Hagan laughed, a sharp barking sound that reminded Borgil of a hyena, and put his teeth on edge.

***

Raining. Corin opened his eyes and wished he hadn't. The brute with the kettle helm was standing over him, urinating.

"Stop that," Corin recognized the voice. *Hagan the Morwellan.* Kettle Helmet laughed and tied his drawstrings. He shuffled off and joined whomever else was with Hagan. Hard to see what's happening behind you when lashed to a thorn bush.

"Hagan," Corin spat out blood. His head felt like a camel had slept on it and his mouth was dry and swollen. Hands tied behind back. Blood, vomit, and piss all over his stolen robe. "Where's my sword?"

Hagan's face appeared. He looked amused. "Back in the land of the living? Good. We're heading back to the city, so I'll bid you good day." Hagan turned away.

"I want my sword back."

'I left it in the *'Duck,'*" Hagan turned and stared at him, the cold gray eyes faintly amused.

"Bring me Clouter," Corin croaked.

"Clouter?" Hagan raised a brow. "Doesn't it deserve a better name than that? Bloody thing's clumsy as a fence post."

"You've had a go with it?" Corin wished he could punch holes in Hagan's face.

"Everyone had a go until Borgil destroyed the taproom counter and the Crimson Elite got word of trouble, we had to hole up next door."

"Who's Borgil?"

"You just met him."

"Oh," Corin felt something crawling across his face. A fly—or worse. "Tell that shithead I'll be seeing him soon."

"Don't think he'll lose much sleep over that," Hagan said.

"He should," Corin said, testing the cords cutting into his wrist. The fly was on his eyelid. It stung him and flew off. Another settled on his cheek.

'Three hours left in the sun—you'll cook nicely," Hagan said. "Best tell me about that gold while you can speak."

"Piss off," Corin said. "I'll get assistance elsewhere. If that arse in the helmet is anything to go by your new friends wouldn't prove much help."

"Borgil? He's unhinged but enthusiastic," Hagan said. "The other lads are alright, except Rejen—I don't like Rej."

"Who's Rej?"

Hagan shook his head as though bored with their chat. "*Gold,* Corin?"

"You won't get any."

"You're upset with me?" Hagan laughed. "Just a prank on a sunny afternoon. The boys were restless so I suggested a trip out to the country. Go visit the flies. Take you with us and deposit you here. Abandoned—like you abandoned me when I first arrived here."

"I didn't think you needed a nurse maid," Corin's stung eye was swelling, he could hardly see through that one.

"I was *hurt*," Hagan said. "Had to start from scratch, my only friend having deserted me."

"Melodramatic."

"Anyway—we're even now, so no hard feelings. Tell me more about this gold—*Please*."

Corin sighed. Two flies were on his face, and something else had bitten his leg. Glancing down he saw ants crawling up his robe. *Sometimes you just have to compromise.* "It's a job," Corin said. "A girl I need to find."

"You'll find plenty in the *'Duck,'*" Hagan said. "Oh, whoops, you're lashed to a tree. Sorry, about that. Some rich man's daughter?"

"Silon of Raleen, my current boss," Corin said, thinking how his prospects of staying employed were getting slimmer by the minute. "His only daughter was kidnapped in Atarios. They're taking her to the Sedinadola slave markets."

"A lot of effort for one girl," Hagan said. He produced a knife and started slicing through Corin's bonds. "Maybe she's dead already."

"She's alive," Corin said rubbing life back into his hands. "That's the point. Silon has powerful enemies. One in particular wants to hurt him, take him apart piece by piece. Nalissa will be sold and Silon will pay a fortune to save her from a fate worse than death."

"I don't know a lot about Sedinadola," Hagan said. "But I've heard that's where the sultan lives with his favorite Crimson Guard, to whom you so kindly introduced me."

"It will prove tricky getting inside the city," Corin nodded. "Why I need assistance."

"You're free," Hagan said. "No offense, but it's been an enjoyable afternoon." He turned away, and called out. "Hey, Boys! Fancy a vacation in the Royal City?' Hagan turned back just in time to catch Corin's punch in his face.

"None taken," Corin told him.

***

Later, back in *The Green Duck,* Corin sat dicing with Hagan and two of his men. Kettle Helm had kept his distance when Corin was reunited with Clouter. Borgil was sulking upstairs somewhere. Corin would pay him a visit later.

"We'll need to get in and out that city several times," Dilan, the one with the eye-patch said. Corin thought him a reasonable fellow, as was Coly the rangy lad with blonde curly hair, an ex-Bear seated beside him. Corin didn't care for the Bears. As an ex-Wolf he had cause, but Coly seemed decent enough. He hadn't been introduced to the others yet. Except Borgil. "We need to know the drill, where the garrisons are," Dilan added.

"And the slave markets," Hagan said. He'd mentioned gold to his men and all of them were keen. Except Dilan who was worried they'd be entering a trap.

"Best set up camp outside the city," Coly said. "We can dress like camel traders, or goat herders. There's no shortage of them fellows lurking outside the cities."

"I suggest you boys get some rest," Corin said shouldering Clouter. "We'll be leaving this city before dawn."

"Where you going?" Hagan looked up seeing Corin about to leave.

"Going to have a chat with your friend Borgil."

The girl yelled as Corin kicked open the door. It wasn't a pretty sight. He nodded and the lass scarpered. Corin loomed over the naked mass of hair covering the bed. "You didn't even take your fucking helmet off?" Corin jumped on top of the bed, which nearly collapsed. He stood over Borgil and kicked him hard in the balls, then he knelt down and grabbed the big man's helmet and lifted Borgil to his feet.

A window was close. Corin, a hand on each horn, introduced Borgil to the wall with a thud and then shoved the yelling naked mercenary out of the window.

Borgil crashed into the street and three hounds were on him before he'd found his feet.

"Cross my path again and I'll slice you in half," Corin shouted at the mess, the dogs growling and barking, men shouting nearby. Corin dusted down his palms. One more drink and he'd retire. Yet another busy day, but Corin suspected tomorrow might prove worse.

Chapter 9 | Two Cities

She glided swift and silent, a white flash passing over sand, the sea flanking her right and a horned moon winking through racing cloud above. Ta-Kai could make out the tall spheres of her destination. A long flight from Syrannos, but it was no problem for her to navigate through the silent dark, just another white owl hunting.

Nalissa would sleep well tonight, Ta-Kai had seen to that. The drugs were strong, purchased at market this morning, and used for subduing beasts or unruly slaves before the whip was needed. She'd left the girl snoring in the room she'd rented in the lower city. No questions asked, two silver coins had paid for sealed lips, she'd hinted the landlord would receive more tomorrow.

Ta-Kai was pleased with her new life. She got to employ her skills freely and was paid handsomely for the pleasure. Caswallon was useful, he'd saved her from those enemies in Shen. A clever man steeped in lore and ancient craft who lacked the weaknesses of most his kind. The sorcerer's fargaze, and cunning spell craft had reached out and pulled her across. An *Aikashi* from Shen—one of the shapeshifters banished and forever trapped in limbo by the treacherous spellcasters of that land.

"'You are free to work as you wish,'" Lord Caswallon had told her in the cold tower far away. Cunning and careful, he'd had no trouble cutting her raging soul free of the invisible spell-bonds holding her. The horror of that limbo was just a memory. A distant noise, a gray nothing. It crept back when she slept, But Ta-kai didn't sleep often. She preferred to fly. *To hunt.*

"'I need to kill,'" she'd answered the sorcerer up in his tower.

"'That's why you're here,'" he'd said. "'But first I need to test your loyalty, *Aikashi*. Your kind are rumored to be capricious.'"

"'I am in your debt," she'd said. "My kind are loyal.'" *Loyal to ourselves and the Lord of the Night, not to mortals—never to you!*

Her client had then informed her what he required. The humiliation then annihilation of a persistent nuisance, a thorn in his side. The Raleenian spice trader called Silon. His daughter Nalissa was just the first step in breaking him. A meddling merchant; a tricky man who could stop Caswallon's ascent. He was High King's councilor, but Ta-Kai suspected Caswallon wanted the throne. Not that she cared. Not her business.

But Ta-Kai had agreed to comply with his wishes. An easy decision. She'd been a captured spirit for so long it was impossible to describe the joy she felt. The glory of hunting, killing, tearing flesh as she had reveled in during that previous time, before the Magister's soldiers had cornered her people and wiped them from the earth.

Ansu was *her* realm, gift of the Night Lord, the *Shadowman*—and had been long before the wretched mortals arrived like so many grubbing insects crawling and multiplying from the mud. The *Aikashi*, her cruel, magnificent race had served their master Old Night for millennia. Witnessed Him fall, then rise again, and fall a second time, crumbling into dust. But Ta-Kai knew He'd return a third time. The Lord of the Shadow. She had only to wait.

The spires were closer, and hazy gold domes capped the crest of the city ahead. A beautiful sight as morning's pink-golden glow spilled light from behind her. A city of alabaster and gold, circular in shape, the streets winding up and up, a corkscrew, toward the central dome, the white, golden-roofed palace surrounded by ornate gardens facing the temple.

She glided close, eased back and settled in those gardens—a leaf descending from branch in a breeze. Ta-Kai alighted beneath palms and shifted back into her preferred human form. A young woman, pale of face, dark-eyed, graceful and lithe—clad in plain black leather. Ta-Kai stretched out her arms and smiled. The man she sought would be waiting close by. She strolled through the gardens as early sunlight woke the birds, and far below the city came to life. Ta-Kai's grin widened; the gardens were beautiful and reminded her of that other place, before the enemy came.

The contact was dressed in a white gown, sandals, and wore a red cap to keep the sun from his shaven bald pate. The second time she'd met this man. Caswallon's spy in the south.

"Selimo," Ta-Kai tilted her head slightly as she approached the chair where the man sat, a scroll balanced on his knees, and small glasses clipping his nose. He looked up, smiled as though overcome with joy at her appearance.

"*Aikashi,* I'm most happy to see you," the man Selimo said. "I've heard you've a gift for me."

"You are misinformed," Ta-Kai said taking seat at the bench beside him. His smile broadened and a fat lazy hand brushed her thigh. She pictured a knife in his eye, but like Caswallon this one had his uses and she would need his cooperation and support.

She shifted, lifted the fat hand off her leg. "The gift is not for you, Merchant, nor for your master in that palace. But rather, my payment for a job well done. My *prize,* my coin."

"You have the merchant's daughter?" Selimo looked around as if expecting the girl to jump out from under a palm.

"In Syrannos—safe and quiet," Ta-Kai said.

A cloud crossed Selimo's congenial features. "That is irregular. I was informed you'd be bringing her here."

"And perhaps I shall, but first I need to find the right vendor. My client was most specific. He wants to hurt this Silon. Break him, and learn all the man knows. That foolish girl is Silon's soft spot. She needs to be sold in the common markets, whipped bloody and used. The word of it must reach the merchant up in Raleen promptly."

"A waste," Selimo wiped sweat from his round face. Already hot despite the earliness of the hour. "Silon is a dangerous man," he said. "You shouldn't underestimate him."

"I don't care," Ta-Kai smiled. "I want flesh and gold. Name me a dealer where I can take her, and then inform my client in the north."

Selimo rubbed his fat chin. "I wish you'd let me handle this, *Aikashi*. I could make the transactions, see to the girl's purchase and settlement."

"I'm to be directly involved—that's what he wants," she said. This fat slug wanted to paw over Nalissa himself, sample the goods. Not going to happen. Compassion wasn't part of an *Aikashi's* makeup. But dislike was and she felt nothing but contempt for the creature beside her on the bench.

She stood gazing down at the moist brown eyes. "Give me a name."

Selimo sighed, wiped his face with a silk cloth retrieved from his pocket. "Dracal," he said eventually. "He's the most feared and respected dealer in Sedinadola."

"Where do I find him?"

"In the desert," Selimo smiled and then tensed as though expecting a blow.

Ta-kai stood over him, her small fists clenched. "Do not test me, fat man—else I rip out your lungs and hang them on those bushes for the birds to peck. *Where?*"

"He has a camp a dozen miles from the city," Selimo was sweating profusely. "People come to Dracal. He prefers to conduct business from his camp, that way he's free from interference by the Crimson Guard. Those boys always want their cut in profits."

"Which direction?"

"Due south. Twelve miles—there's an oasis of sorts, you'll see the birds. I-"

Ta-Kai left Selimo sitting with his mouth open, the sweat beading from his face. "Lie to me, Slug and I'll find you in the dark," she flicked a dark blade through her fingers then stowed it in her tunic, a sweeping motion faster than he could follow. Ta-Kai smiled at the fear in his eyes. She stole away, pacing off into the shroud of green surrounding the courtyard, vanishing like mist chased by morning sun.

***

Nalissa woke at the sound of scraping at her window. She blinked, looked over to where the morning sun stabbed at her from the open shutters. Something fluttered. *A bird?* She blinked again, then the shutters slammed shut banishing the light and her captor's pale face emerged from the gloom.

"I trust you're well rested?" the woman smiled at her, not a warm smile. More like a glint of satisfaction at a task well done.

"I dreamed of bats, dark shadowy creatures flying around my head," Nalissa said. Her eyes were heavy as stones and the room was moving slightly. "I don't feel..."

"That will wear off," the woman said sitting beside her on the bed and brushing cold fingers through her hair. Nalissa shivered at that touch, something of the night within it. "We need to leave soon," her captor said, her white hand dropping to cup Nalissa's breast. She held her breath and the woman, noticing her tension laughed cruelly.

"You *are* a beauty—why so shy?"

"Where am I?" Nalissa wished her head felt better. Something had been done to her. Had she been drunk? No, a different feeling. *Groggy.* This vile woman had drugged her. Nalissa felt sudden horror. *What else has she done?*

"In a city, about to leave for another," the woman rose to her feet and gazed down at Nalissa. "I will bring food and water, you'll need to be ready in half an hour."

"Ready for what?"

"A journey, my dear."

"I still don't know your name," Nalissa felt a vague memory, a word spoken.

"I told you on the ship three nights ago," the woman smiled at her again and then faded through the room, the sound of doors opening and shutting behind her.

Nalissa swung her legs free of the bed and stood. A mistake, her legs buckled and she fell face-first onto the floorboards. She wept in frustration and struck the wood with her small fists. What had that bitch done to her?

Father — where are you? She staggered to her knees, and slowly, far more carefully rose to her feet, hands gripping the table beside her. She counted to ten. the room was solid, her vision was clearing. And her temper returning.

How dare she…?

Nalissa kicked the table across the room sending it careering into a wall. She kicked it again and then punched a hole in the plaster. *I'm going to cut your fucking eyes out!* The rage felt good but it was soon replaced by a terrible loneliness and dread of what was coming.

Slave.

She walked over to the shutters, pulled them back allowing the day back in. Noises reached her, carts wheeling through the lane below, voices laughing, others angry. Dogs growling, somewhere nearby an infant crying.

And the smells… Night soil, stale vomit, the stench of rotting fish, vinegar hinting spilled wine, and something far worse—a decaying corpse perhaps? She looked out best she could; the window allowed small purchase. Nalissa saw a narrow street angling down a slope toward a cluster of buildings, the masts of boats bobbing visible beyond. That explained the fish smell. She was near the docks. Perhaps in a tavern of sorts.

Cappel Cormac. Father had people here, owned property. There was still a chance. She wedged open the window, and heedless of her scant garments dangled her legs above the street. She leapt free, falling fifteen, maybe twenty foot onto cobbles and yelling as her ankle twisted painfully and she bruised her knee.

Fuck!

Nalissa pulled the shift close about her person, hardly adequate, and no shoes. She must look like a waif, a mad woman. She ran best she could—more of a hobble—down to the distant wharfs where she glimpsed the blue of water. *And escape!*

A man emerged, glared at her. She heard someone laughing behind. Nalissa stumbled on, the morning closing on her and the noise of the docks getting louder. She reached a corner, rested her hands against a wall and drew in deep breaths. She saw the water, sunlight reflecting as light danced.

Another shout. A man blocked her way. Big, scarred, a smile smudging his swarthy features. He reached for her, but Nalissa's kick caught him neatly in the balls. She elbowed his ear and then fell on top of him, found her feet again and stumbled on toward the docks.

She heard gulls crying, saw their white shapes racing through the blue above. She was close. A ship—that was all she needed. Her father was known here. Not liked but known. And gold always paved the way.

Nalissa reached the harbor, took a turn and then cried out when a blow from nowhere knocked her on her back. Her head struck the pavers and she spewed again. A face loomed over her, reddish beard, earing in left ear. Another face, gap tooth, tattoo on cheek, long black greasy hair. A third man loomed closer, but his face she couldn't see.

"Look what we've found," the bearded face grinned down at her."

"I'm Silon's daughter," Nalissa said. "He'll pay gold."

"Gold?" Redbeard's eyes widened, and then widened further when the pointed tip of a blade emerged suddenly from his throat. He fell on her his blood soaking her face.

Nalissa screamed, yelled, and rolled free. Someone kicked her onto her face, then kicked her again. She heard a brief clash of steel, a man's scream. Another's. Then ice cold hands as strong as wire pulled her to her feet.

Nalissa stared into her captor's callous eyes. "We've a journey to make," the woman said slapping her face. "Try that again and I'll take an ear, maybe an index finger too. Neither will affect your price." That iron grip twisted her around and Nalissa was pushed forward, forced to stagger back up the lane she'd abandoned. She saw men staring, their faces alarmed, scared even. *Cowardly bastards!*

An hour later Nalissa was strapped face down across a mule, her damp eyes watching them close the city gates behind her. She'd heard her captor telling the guards she was the daughter of a traitor and would be sold next week in Sedinadola, or perhaps ritually beheaded—whatever the Sultan prescribed. He wasn't fond of traitors.

Body hurting, vomit clinging to her face, and tears wept dry, Nalissa closed her eyes and prayed this was a nightmare she'd wake from soon. They left the city behind, her captor's horse clomping ahead and the pony following.

Nalissa drifted in and out of thoughts, her aching body and despair fading into dreaminess. A face floated before her. Beautiful and mysterious. A woman with flowing chestnut hair and haunting eyes of green and gold. The dream-woman smiled at her, and her husky voice spoke in whispers evoking memory of springtime mornings in a wood near her home.

Have courage. He will find you in time…

The woman's face vanished, the dream image too. Nalissa heard thunder rolling—or was it hoofbeats? She saw another face, hard blue-gray eyes. A rider, dust trailing behind his horse. A longsword was strapped across his back.

Corin!

He will find you in time…

***

Dracal watched the night birds peck the eyes from his latest victim. A man who'd dared to gainsay his wishes. An important man—once. Now a screaming, gibbering mess of blood and torn flesh. An evening's entertainment in his camp beneath the stars.

It was late. The moon high above spilled silver on the camp and its surroundings. Dracal was weary. Time to retire. Bored of his game, the slave trader rose to his feet and slipped his curved dagger free of it sheath. He smiled at his captive briefly and then slashed his throat wide open. The man gurgled, faded into nothing. Another corpse for the desert.

Food for the wild dogs and hyenas, together with the slaves he'd butchered yesterday. Old men no longer useful, their limbs and tongues removed, their bodies staked out in the sun. Anything to relieve the monotony of desert camp in late summer.

Tomorrow he'd ride back into the city, meet with his contact and then make for the ships to see what new merchandise was available.

Dracal smiled; he was the richest man outside Sedinadola. Of course, he could live in the city should he wish to, and the sultan would turn a blind eye to his affairs.

But Dracal was desert born, and the nomad life was in his blood. He was the lord of this camp, owing nothing to anyone. And the Crimson Guard had no power out here.

He strolled over to his marquee, made ready by his slaves, three women and two men. Each skilled at the tasks he required from them.

The dark girl, Ranysi, appeared naked, her smooth skin glinting in the firelight. Dracal wasn't in the mood. He dismissed her with a flick of his hand. One of the male slaves appeared and removed his slippers, lit his pipe and placed it in his master's hands. Dracal pulled the sweet fumes down deep into his lungs, leaning back, allowing the familiar contentment fill his head.

The slaves readied his quarters and vanished, leaving him to his thoughts. Dracal leaned back in his wicker chair, rocking slightly, the smoke trailing up through the hole in the top of the canvas.

A full hour he sat there, dreaming, smoking...*drifting*. Then started upright when the figure emerged in front of his eyes. *A woman.* She held a dagger to his throat.

"I'm bringing you someone." The face was pale, those eyes feral, cold. Unusual "You will meet me in the city in one week and pay the sum I require." The knife left his throat and hovered an inch from his eye.

Dracal spoke quietly. He was a brave man, and no fool. Whoever had sent this assassin had overstepped the line. But for now, he'd play their game. "What do I get from the purchase?"

"A girl," the woman said, and Dracal noticed how deathly pale her skin seemed in the lantern light.

"That it?"

"It's all you need to know for now," she said. "Look for my return in a few days, and prepare to meet me in the city." She faded back from the light, and in his foggy state he lost sight of her.

Gone. Dracal cursed softly and rose to his feet. A slave appeared, but he waved him away, reached for the drapes and squeezed through. Outside he saw stars, the moon, its reflection on the water close by. Palms brushed in breeze, and a dark speck shot up startling him like a crossbow bolt vanishing north.

A bird? Hard to say. Dracal gazed down – there were no footprints, no ground disturbance. He saw no horse or camel, or sign of anything amiss. Close by the dying fire spat faggots, a dull glow of red.

Disgusted and angry, Dracal glanced around a final time and climbed back inside his tent. He'd order a different brand of weed tomorrow. This last batch was affecting his head in ways he hadn't experienced before.

Chapter 10 | The Strand Again

Corin woke with a jolt and rolled free of the bunk he'd crashed on. The room was empty, his garments thrown over a lone chair, his cloak on the floor. Clouter leaning against the door, barring sudden entry from Borgil or anyone else. He'd slept heavily, a drunken slumber. But woken sharp.

I'm not alone. Corin turned slowly, saw the blinds flicker. And then her face appeared, seemed to float across to him. *Vervandi.* The woman who haunted his dreams, and sometimes crept outside them. Her face was hard to define, drifting in and out like smoke in a breeze.

Corin drank in those green/gold eyes, the perfect visage, the long wavy copper cascade that framed her features and tumbled over her shoulders. Vervandi.

"Am I still sleeping or are you real?" Corin rubbed his eyes, blinked. She remained. Clearer now, standing by the window, clad in her customary green. Tall, willowy, those mercurial eyes sad and distant.

"You look older," she said, her voice husky but remote, as though she were speaking from another room, *or another world.* The world where the creatures living inside dreams stole upon those daring to sleep. A perilous place where a man could lose his soul.

"Well worn," Corin coughed. "And in better condition than last I saw you."

"Yet, no wiser."

"I'm a swordsman not a seer, so spare me your scrutiny." Corin stared hard at that face. *Why are you here?*

"Be careful," Vervandi said. "lest you clumsy hunters become prey."

"You mean the Lynx," Corin said. "I'm already wary of that one."

"You haven't a notion what you're dealing with."

"I'll work it out, and I've help from the lads downstairs," Corin hinted the door where Clouter leaned. "It's a task I've been given— no way out."

"There is always a way out if you find it early enough. But for you it may be too late. You *must* save that girl, Corin," the woman said, her slender arm resting against the window frame. "We cannot allow Silon to become vulnerable. He is key to our survival."

"Who is *we?*" Corin said, strange how he'd become so relaxed during her visitations. The dream woman who'd haunted him since boyhood. Vervandi was part of him now. And she had saved him from swinging that day. But why bother? Who was Corin to her? That part he'd never worked out. *What's so special about me?*

"The players in this game," she said, her beautiful face turning to the window. "You are the Gray Wolf, Corin. My favorite survivor, a small but important part of the jigsaw. Silon the merchant is another piece in the puzzle. We cannot afford to lose either of you."

"I always get the feeling you help me for your own reasons and I might have to pay a high price sometime. And I can never remember the details after you leave me. Why is that?"

"I erase your memory," she smiled, and he remembered how that smile cut through his swiftly-built defenses quicker than cold steel through flesh.

"That's kind of you."

"For your own sake. You need to stay focused," She said, turning again. Her eyes locking onto his, the ghost of whimsical smile fleeing from her lips. Outside a glimmer of light promised dawn. "I need to leave," Vervandi said. "Like your adversary, I'm a creature of the night."

"Tell me of this Lynx woman?"

"She is an *Aikashi*, a spirit from the old world. A servant of Old Night and Chaos."

"*A what?*" Corin pictured the girl—Tashi—in Rado's inn. Suddenly things made sense. *A demon.*

"She is half in this world and half in Yffarn. The *Aikashi* were a cruel race, who were defeated and cast out by the conjurers of Shen and the dark gods they worshipped. The Shen paid a high price for their actions." Her face was fading as she spoke and Corin felt that familiar yearning.

The room was getting lighter and the tall, willowy woman fading fast from his eyes. "And she can fly," Corin said, his heart thumping in his chest. "The demon wench can fly."

"An *Aikashi* will find you anywhere if they need too. Stay awake, watch every shadow," her voice lingered though her face had faded like mist in sunshine. "The man who summoned her knows you work for his enemy. Thus you, Corin an Fol are in peril too."

"Caswallon, the High King's councilor? I don't think he's heard of me," Corin said. But Vervandi had gone replaced by warm sunlight and lost memories, these torn apart by a loud knocking on his door.

"Trust no one, sleep with one eye open…" Her whispers reached him from far away. His mind drifted then the knocking came again.

Fuck it.

Corin leaped to his feet and stubbed a toe on a floor nail. Cussing, he thumped the door. "Who's there?"

"Hagan."

"What?"

"What do you mean—what? It's frigging daylight and you wanted to get started early as I recall."

"Well, fine—just give me a minute," Corin reached for his hose and boots.

"Take your time," Hagan said. "We might as well wait until every trader and peddler in this shithole is clogging the lanes." There was the sound of boots trailing off downstairs. Corin dressed, strapped Clouter to his harness, threw the cloak over his shoulders and pinned it with his wolf broach.

"You can't lug that thing all the way to Sedinadola," Hagan said when Corin joined the others in the common room. Some of the *Duck's* girls had breakfast going and Corin tucked into rice and bacon, figs spiced with cumin.

Corin stowed Clouter against the table, saw Borgil glaring at him and winked at Kettle Helm. "Morning, Shithead," Corin said, and Borgil turned away.

"You shouldn't provoke him," Hagan said quietly. Then he tapped Clouter's pommel. "You need a smaller sword, I'm thinking. Might get noticed with that."

"I'll lean on it—pretend it's a staff," Corin said then chewed at his bacon. Someone brought coffee and he took a slurp, burning his mouth.

"Yeah—that will work," Hagan said. "Particularly if you strap a sign to it saying, 'Beggar Man Stay Clear.'"

"I'm not going anywhere without my longsword," Corin said, closing the matter.

"So, what's the plan?" Hagan said.

"Camels," Corin munched and sipped, more carefully this time. "Already got 'em."

"What?"

"Coly and Dol bought nine this morning, got to the markets before sunrise."

"Fast work," Corin was impressed.

"They'll have them ready for us at the west gate. So…what's our plan?"

"We'll need disguises, so we blend in," Corin said.

"Dilan bought desert robes and djellabas so we'll blend in very nicely, apart from your fucking sword. *Our…plan?*"

"Ride to Sedinadola and save that girl," Corin said, "That's my plan, Hagan. Best I can do before fucking breakfast."

They had no problem leaving the city because of everyone else trying to get in. Beggars, traders, peddlers, merchants and camel sellers all clustered like blowflies around the gates.

Dressed in their desert garb, Corin, Hagan and the others forced their way through the throng and made for the corrals where Coly and Dol waited with the camels.

"How do you ride those things?" Hagan asked Corin as they each grabbed a beast's harness.

"You don't," Corin said. "You climb on their back and try not to fall off." His camel spat at him, clearly this was the start of a good relationship.

"Think she likes you," Coly laughed. Corin had purchased a rug, a cheap shabby affair that concealed Clouter, tied longways across his camel. Not pretty, but it worked.

They rode throughout that day, sweltering, the sun's glare bouncing off the crushed shells comprising *The Silver Strand.*

"We had best avoid Syrannos," Corin told Hagan and Coly riding along side.

They passed some traveling merchants and Coly waved. "Don't

do that," Hagan said. "We don't want trouble if we can avoid it."

"Just blending in," Coly said.

"Don't bother," Corin said. "They're miserable bastards here. The only friendly ones are trying to sell you something." At dusk they camped on the side of the strand, hidden by dunes, their campfire one of several winking under the sky.

Corin strolled free of the camp to have a moment in the bushes. That done, he wandered back down to *The Silver Strand*, running empty for miles either side. A clear night, starry and silent, save the distant rumble of breakers on sand a half mile north.

Edgy, Corin climbed the nearest dune and saw the campfires studding the horizon like glowing serpents' eyes. He tried not to think about Vervandi and what she had said—as ever the memory had become hazy after she'd left.

A flying assassin. Not good news—and also some kind of demon creature out of nightmare. Poor Nalissa. Corin felt for that girl, spirited lass though she was she'd need every ounce of that grit.

Hagan was right, he didn't have a plan. Things evolved when you kept moving. Staying alive, work through one problem, check that and on to the next. Doesn't pay to look too far ahead. That said he was gloomy tonight. Seeing Vervandi always unraveled him. She'd always been there, in the background. Like a guardian watching over him. *But why?* She'd hinted he was part of something much bigger, and Silon too. That wasn't overly comforting.

And that villain Caswallon was part of the pattern. Best not dwell on that aspect. He needed a practical solution for their project, else things would break apart before they reached Sedinadola—still a week's ride ahead.

No point stopping at Syrannos searching for clues. Avoid the hornet and make straight for the nest. Sedinadola. They needed to leave *The Silver Strand* at some point before they were in sight of

Syrannos. A cut across the desert, hopefully not a long one, then they'd set up camp near the sultan's city.

He would take a snoop. Creep in under dark, or maybe in full daylight among the cluster of stinking traders. Probably a better option, should Cappel Cormac be an example.

But how to find Nalissa? Simple—scan the slave markets. He'd bring Hagan with him, Coly too. Corin liked Coly, not a bad lad. Bright. The others would wait in camp, especially Borgil who was ugly enough to get them all killed in Corin's opinion.

We'll grab a slaver, work the knife on him until he squeaks. Corin smiled as his plan took shape. He wandered back into camp, nodded to Hagan still crouched by the fire. Lumps in blankets told him the others were sleeping.

"You're a restless bastard," Hagan said.

"It's kept me alive," Corin crouched beside him and sipped from the offered water gourd.

"Could use an ale and a smoke," Hagan said leaning back against a rock. His gray eyes narrowed. "There's something you're not telling us about this business."

"Like what?"

"I don't know," Hagan said. "You're being cagey, like you know something we don't."

"We're stalking a female winged assassin," Corin told him and Hagan rolled back laughing.

"You're a piece of work, Corin an Fol," Hagan said. "I'll see you in the morning." Corin watched him wander off and roll tight in his blanket, snores joining the others minutes later.

Well you did fucking ask. Corin stared at the fire's glow, and then looked up at the myriad stars, a diadem of glittering buttons studding the void. So quiet. Just the distant sound of breakers, the earth turning beneath his feet. Being part of something bigger made a man feel very small.

Chapter 11 | The Harbor at Dusk

Dracal examined the stock with critical eyes. Prisoners. Victims of conflict, caught in the crossfire. Tired, half dead things. A row of twenty, chained together, limping, bloody—not much use for anything.

"You giving these away?" Dracal said to the portly trader captain from the nearby galley docked at the end of the jetty. His ship was fresh from Yamondo in the far south. The slaver had sold most of his trade and was looking to finish up business for the day. Dracal had heard Yamondo was at war with its neighbor Vendel. A long-running bloody business. Didn't concern him, distant places, jungle realms somewhere beyond Golt. *Who cares.*

I'll take two dozen in silver," the man said.

Dracal grabbed his collar.

"Don't insult me—these cretins are half dead already. A day's work and they'll prove a feast for flies. You should pay me for dragging them off you."

The slaver looked weary, not in the mood to fight. "Give me ten in silver," he said. "They'll freshen up with some water and rest. Most should last a few months, if you treat them right. Good deal you have there."

"I'd need more than water to freshen these sorry fuckers," Dracal reached over and pulled one of the fettered captives toward him. The man just stared, glazed expression, dead eyes. Dracal slapped his face. *No response*, so he whipped out his curved dagger and cut a slice from an ear, the blood trickled, still no response.

"Six silver pieces," the slaver said, his dark eyes on the blood dripping from the captive's ear. Dusk was approaching. Dracal knew the captain had to get back to his vessel before curfew. The Crimson Guard would be here soon. Not a problem for Dracal; he had the license. The Sultan's Elite turned a blind eye to his actions. They saw it as an uncomfortable necessity. As long as Dracal operated from his camp, he could trade at the docks, get fresh stock whenever needed. Everyone gained from that. The slave trade was thriving in the Royal City.

"Three," Dracal turned, saw the Guard filing out of the gates, spears slanted over shoulders, armor gleaming, red cloaks ironed and pressed. The galley captain saw them too. He looked pained, but nodded reluctantly.

"You are robbing me."

Dracal took three silver pennies from his pouch and placed them in the slaver's fat palm. The man glared at him and turned away, pacing briskly back to his galley, the sun sinking like a bloodstone into water far behind.

Dracal smiled. The slaver had been right, this fresh batch would survive after rest and sustenance. He'd keep them for a week or so and then sell them on, save for a few he'd use for entertainment in the camp.

He called his three men over. His steward, overseer, and the camp physician always accompanied Dracal to the markets and docks. They'd been dealing with the last traders from other vessels at the far side of the quay, purchased a few female captives brought in from further along the coast. A raid on some village apparently.

"Take this lot away. Feed and water them, and patch up that one's ear," Dracal told the steward. "I want them fit for work in the morning." His second nodded and, together with the other two, cracked their whips, and kicked, punched and pushed the filthy exhausted column into motion. Dracal watched on with disgust until the miserable sight had left his eyes. He turned. Surveyed the water, the distant palms, the red sheen on the horizon.

They'd done well today, sold twenty slaves for a good profit to the sultan's dealer in the city. And neither the women or those chained wretches had cost overmuch. He should be content. Instead something was nagging him.

Dracal heard a slight creak on the jetty behind. He turned, started when a figure emerged on the gangway blocking him. A distortion of light and shadow, like a heat haze aura it hurt his eyes. The shape solidified and fused into a woman striding briskly toward him. *Her.* Not a dream as he'd hoped.

"Did you forget our arrangement?" She had stopped several feet away. Balanced, poised, two swords slung across her back their hilts showing above each shoulder. Clad in leather, arms folded neatly, leather wrist straps barbed with small daggers. Her dark eyes were unsettling in the fading light. Dracal glimpsed beyond, saw the afterglow reflected on the Crimson's armor. Time to inspect the docks. The Guard would be here in minutes.

"I thought you a dream," Dracal smiled, masking his alarm. She *had* been a dream until this moment, a nightmare he'd tried to forget. Blamed it on the smoke, had the supplier flayed over coals. He'd never had visions before.

"Who are you?"

"You can call me the Lynx." There was something suggestive in the woman's smile. She peeled her lips back farther and Dracal noticed the neatly filed teeth. He felt a stab of fear, tried pushing past.

"I've a gift," she said, blocking him. "You need to come and claim it, else our deal is off."

"I know of no deal, or arrangement," Dracal said, irritated, and angry with himself because of the fear cramping his belly. "You were in my camp—*somehow*. Creeping about. Who do you work for?"

"Myself," she showed those teeth again, *disturbing*. "Though I contract out a lot. I have the girl at the gates outside the city. Tethered," she smiled again. "You're going to like to like her, Dracal. A handful."

"I already have girls in my camp—more than I need."

"This one is different, more of a hostage. A valuable piece in a game being played out. You get to display her for a time, lure in the bait. The real prize."

Dracal was intrigued despite his trepidations. Who was this terrifying woman and—more importantly—who did she work for? He needed answers quickly. The Guard had seen them and were marching over.

"You had better leave," Dracal nodded at the six Crimson cloaked soldiers who had broken off from the main squad and were tromping down through the harbor and dockyard, their faces hard, angry and suspicious.

"You there!" The corporal called across to Dracal. "Wrap up your business and depart, else you'll get a flogging."

"I have a permit," Dracal fumbled in his pouch and produced the voucher, annoyed at the corporal's arrogance. He waved it in the air, the woman beside him watched the exchange with an amused expression. Confident bitch.

Dracal hated the Crimson Guard, but so did everyone. *The Sultan's special boys.* The interruption was inconvenient; he had to find out what this woman wanted. There could be gold in it, though he suspected there'd be danger too. He looked up, light was fading fast, the water, silver and smooth in the harbor beyond, a few vessels bobbing gently.

The corporal clattered onto the jetty where Dracal stood alongside the strange woman called the Lynx. She seemed disinterested in the Crimson Guard. The corporal noticed her manner and rounded on Dracal. He seized the docket, his five spearmen gathered around. The corporal glared at the details and nodded tensely.

"You are good to go," he said shoving the docket back in Dracal's palm.

Dracal stowed the permit away and smiled. "Just finishing up," he said, "be done in twenty." Dracal pointed to the other end of the jetty where his overseer and physician could be seen checking over the new purchases, probing, prodding, and jabbing the scrawny wretches chained in the line. "Almost done," Dracal added as the corporal hadn't moved, and his five men were leveling spears.

Come on. Dracal waved his hands to placate.

"Who is this?" The corporal had bared his steel. The scimitar glinted, the shine matching his cloak and trapping the last of the dying sunlight. He raised it at the woman. "Your business, *wench?*"

An unfortunate choice of words. Dracal saw how the aloof distant expression on her face turned to rage. A feral, terrifying savagery even he hadn't encountered before.

"What did you call me?" The voice was a hiss, a cat snarl. *A threat.*

"Seize her!" The corporal said, and his spearmen closed in.

***

Nalissa jolted awake hearing shouts and the sound of wheels grinding to a stop. They'd reached their destination. Outside the walls the caravan settled in the for the night. They'd be allowed in the city once the priests had called the morning prayers to Telcanna the Sky God, the deity worshipped above all others down here in Permio.

The caravan had left Syrannos, a boisterous train of camels, carts and donkeys, the odd horse. These were guided and ridden by men working for merchants and traders, mostly with goods to sell in the Sultan's city.

Amidst that colorful troop, was a battered looking rental carriage with three guards sat dicing outside with the driver, the horses tethered behind. Hidden in the carriage, the drapes pulled back, Nalissa saw just enough to glimpse sandstone walls shifting from dun, through mocha, then deepening to purple as light changed and then faded into nighttime.

Her guards diced quietly. A sober troop. Hardly surprising; Nalissa's companion had that effect on most men. She'd left an hour or so earlier. Slipped inside the city. Nalissa heard her telling the men she'd business to conduct that couldn't wait until morning.

The carriage was tight on space, hot and dusty, and the long ride had exhausted her. She needed sleep but couldn't settle. The silk scarfs binding her wrists were making her irritable, though it would have been far worse with rope.

Nalissa was trussed and gagged so expertly she could hardly move her head. She managed just enough to see the odd star winking up in the firmament.

Father — where are you?

Anger and rage. Fear—sometimes terror. And, worse a cold clear realism sinking inside her. *I'm destined for slavery.* The thought was like lead weights choking her, pulling her down a black bottomless well, sinking towards despair. But Nalissa wouldn't descent to that pit. Not yet.

There was more to this than making her suffer. It was business, the Lynx kept saying. A contract; she was the hook. They wanted Father. Silon the merchant had a great many enemies, and one of those wanted to hurt him badly.

That meant hurting his daughter. The proud and beautiful Nalissa. Beloved socialite of Atarios's favored circle. Life of the party, breaker of hearts and dreams. Carefree, selfish and spoilt.

Until now.

Father wasn't a fool. He'd know the woman's client would want him to dive in, send people for his daughter. They'd be waiting. *She'd be waiting.* Nalissa's secret sister. The killer known as the Lynx.

She'd heard the bodyguard the woman purchased near Syrannos talking about them in hushed whispers. Two sisters, one sick. The other some kind of warrior from a distant land. She paid them well. The whispers never left their group.

A night breeze brushed the side of her carriage. Out there a horse kicked at sand. The men were quiet. Maybe sleeping? Nalissa had heard them talk about the Lynx once or twice, hinting at who—or what—she was. That hadn't been comforting to hear.

And where was she and what doing? Nalissa had long cried out her tears. Useless things, frustration served her better. *Rage.* Play their game, but at some point she'd have to escape. Death by starvation and thirst in the desert would be better than servicing some fat Permian's cock. She'd cut her throat before letting that happen.

Or better, cut their throats. It was so hard, here inside this creaky cage. Her thoughts like steely blades jabbing fear and dread at her, the silence and dark creeping into her isolated world.

She tugged at the silk cords, not for the first time. She was held fast; her feet were lashed too. She had cramp, lifted a buttock, shifted, turned her head again.

Where are you?

Nalissa craned her neck, glimpsed movement outside. Probably one of the horses. A horned moon spilled silver over sand, she could see campfires winking, heard their crackle in the distance.

She heard the clash of steel—men fighting inside the city. Then a scream tore the night open making her jump, and the night beasts answered from the desert.

***

It happened so fast his blink almost missed it. A blur of steel; the knife slicing throats, stabbing, and men crying out. Dying. Falling with torn throats into the dark water surrounding them.

Dracal had ducked instinctively when the corporal lunged. There'd been no need. His corpse was floating in the harbor as were two of his men, their crimson cloaks mixing with the darker stain of blood.

The three still on the jetty backed away slowly, spears ready. She advanced like a stalking beast of prey. Dracal saw a dancer poised to strike. A creature of the night in her lethal element. The Lynx pounced forward, struck once, twice. A spearman fell to his knees, the weapon clattering beside him.

She danced past, hoisted the spear from the ground with a flick of her hand and blocked the second man's thrust. She reversed the spear and brought it up hard under his neck lifting him off his feet before spinning the spear again, and bringing the point up hard, stabbing him in the groin. The guard pitched screaming into the water, to bob and float alongside his corporal and companions.

That left one. He turned, fled the jetty but the Lynx's knife found him at the end and he fell face first into an abandoned stall.

Silence.

Dracal heard the drip of blood as it spilled from the jetty strakes and plopped into water. Six dead men — all Crimson, and him in the midst. The main squad had moved on, but they'd be back, and quickly if they'd heard those screams. And surely the entire city heard those men scream.

Caught halfway between horror and fascination, Dracal watched the woman calmly walk along the jetty and retrieve her knife from the back of her last victim. She stowed the weapon, purloined an abandoned spear and gazed back, beckoning him to follow.

"In case the rest show an interest," she said, "It's time we left." She turned and jumped down from the jetty, her quick strides fading into dark. Dracal stood transfixed by what had happened. He heard a noise, saw one of his men watching from across the harbor, and motioned him to flee.

They didn't need to be here. There would be more murder soon. Someone held to account. *Not me.*

Dracal ran, adrenaline and fear finally shaking him into action. He saw her shape gliding along the harborside, fading off behind buildings, a ghost sent by the Shadowman himself.

Dracal broke into a sprint when he heard the first shouts announcing the rest of the Guard had seen the corpses of their comrades. He ran full pelt, at last catching up with the woman.

She turned, awarded him a savage grin. "I enjoyed that," she told him, her loping gait like a wolf's running beside him. "It's good to vent."

"You signed our fucking death warrant!" Dracal hissed at her. They'd reached the poor quarter, the shouting on the docks had faded in the distance. "Those Guard will scour every corner of the lower city for what you've done."

"So they'll earn their pay for a change," she smiled at him, a flash of white in the murk.

"There's nowhere to hide," Dracal said.

"You need to find somewhere," she said. "I'll expect to see you in your camp tomorrow."

She cut down a side alley. Disappeared.

He followed. A dead end. No sign of her. "Hide? Where...?"

"Your problem." The voice came from above his head. Dracal

looked up and wished he hadn't. He saw a shape, what appeared to be dark wings stretching out. Then a shadow like that of a giant bat brushed over his head and faded from view lingering like a nightmare creeping into morning.

Dracal dropped to his knees and stayed put for several minutes. At last he recovered enough strength to find his feet again and make for the one place he knew he'd be safe. Those former smuggling days would save him. He found the sewers, climbed through that broken drain he'd used decades before, and dropped down into the stench.

***

Nalissa heard the sound of wingbeats approaching. A rattle and hiss, something settling on the ground nearby. The horses were kicking, and further away other creatures crying out again. Someone shouted a challenge, then nothing. The horse settled and silence reclaimed the camp.

Closer, she could hear one of the men snoring. The carriage door opened and the Lynx stood smiling at her.

"Sleep well?" The woman said. There was blood on her clothes and a savage glint in her eyes.

"I need to…"

"There's a pot outside," the Lynx untied her wrist and ankles, fussing like a caring mother. "Poor child, holding it in all this time."

After she was done, Nalissa returned to the carriage where the woman watched her with those terrible eyes.

"What happened?" Nalissa found herself saying.

"Fools happened," the Lynx said, and then curled up close to her as though they were lovers. The prick of steel against her thigh a subtle reminder that escape was off, for the moment at least.

She slept eventually. The morning sun woke her, and she could hear the woman and guards already busy outside.

"Wake up, Dreamy Girl." The Lynx appeared and pulled back the drapes. "A big day today," she said. "You'll meet your new master, providing he escaped the city. There was some discord in the night I hear." She leaned forward, touching Nalissa's thigh, her eyes huge in the gloom. Nalissa shuddered as the woman ran her bloodstained fingers along the length of her leg, squeezing, kneading, and caressing. Sliding further up. "I've satisfied one hunger," the Lynx said, her voice silk-soft and dangerous.

"Please, not this."

The Lynx struck her face hard with a slap. "You dare reject me?" She snarled, her lips drawn back and Nalissa noticed her teeth had changed from the perfect molars to razor incisors dripping blood.

She cried out, couldn't hold the terror back. But the second blow silenced her. The Lynx stood over Nalissa snarling like a rabid beast, her mouth salivating. "You know nothing about me," she said, her eyes tortured, distorted. "Nothing!" She slammed her teeth together as though denying their existence. The next time Nalissa caught a glimpse those molars were back to normal.

***

Last night had been filled with screams and the clatter of clashing steel. Dracal, hidden in his culvert, had heard marching squads battering down doors, shouting, dragging sleepers into the streets above and hacking them apart.

Sometime after dawn the fuss died down. He slipped out through the drain, filthy and exhausted, a beggar crawling into the streets. He found a corpse lying with throat cut from ear to ear. *Wrong place, wrong time.* A merchant perhaps; the clothes were in good shape, though bloodstained. *And almost my size.*

Dracal dragged the corpse over to a midden, and swiftly stripped the body and dressed in the dead man's gear. He kept his dagger, found another tucked inside the secret stitching in the lining of the corpse's robe.

A dog growled and snapped at him, smelling blood. Dracal rose, kicked at it and the beast whimpered off into a corner. He had to get out of the city—and quickly. The Guard's initial reaction had been to murder anyone. Walking briskly, Dracal saw plenty of evidence with bodies strewn in streets and market squares.

The Guard would be at council now, the Sultan himself alerted to the atrocity down in the docks. They'd do some digging and Dracal's name would emerge. He needed to be back in his camp before that happened.

He knew Sedinadola better than most, found the nearest gate without any difficulty. There were already crowds gathered as the morning traders tussled to get in. He mingled, elbowed and stabbed his way through the gates, buried beneath the throng forcing their way in.

The guards seemed distracted. They clearly had other things on their mind. As he stole from the gates, Dracal turned. He saw a black bird circle and settle on the wall above. A raven. It hopped up onto one of the heads spiked up there and pecked out an eye.

Three heads. Dracal knew one of them. His steward. The other two were damaged beyond recognition.

Chapter 12 | The Camp

Stealing a horse had been easy. Dracal had approached the nearest caravan camp; there were three sprawled less than quarter of a mile from the city walls, the roads, fields and rough terrain all teeming with people. No problem blending in, becoming invisible in the crowd.

Dracal felt dazed and shattered. He hadn't fully digested last night's harrowing events, there was simply too much to absorb. Six Crimson Guard were dead, and before long the suspects would be narrowed down. It was only a matter of time before they held him culpable.

Speed was the key to survival. Fast thinking and moving swiftly. He filtered into the nearest camp, just another trader. A few eyes flicked his way but most were focused on their busy morning. Besides the camp was almost empty with every trader, merchant, thief and camel seller clustering around the gates.

It was always like this in Sedinadola. The three great coastal cities traded back and forth. But whereas Cappel Cormac and Syrannos exported and imported with enthusiasm, the Sultan's city was chary with its possessions—the line stopped here.

The odd bold traveler would fare west for Golt and those little-known places beyond. Brave fools; they seldom returned. The one road leading that way was usually deserted, its crumbling pavers more than half buried under drifting sands.

Dracal found a corral. Both groom and horsemaster were sleeping. Careless, that. He slit their throats, released all the beasts and took the strongest looking, walking the animal through the camp so as not to draw attention, then mounting the beast and riding at speed along the south road making for his camp, his mind racing with plans as the morning wore on and desert heat blazed down like judgment.

***

Ralco Ren Daul had a reputation that surpassed even his master for cruelty. He liked to strip the slaves, whip them bloody and then use them for various purposes. Dracal tolerated his giant mute because Ralco was good at his job. Slaves never escaped. Or if they did they were always re-captured, and the punishments Ralco administered were so imaginative they ensured the rest stayed put.

He was out supervising the women as they carried water back from the small oasis just outside their camp. Ralco never went to the city. Not for him the bustle and mayhem; he'd end up killing people and would swing for the pleasure. Best he stayed put too. Watch over the stock.

It was a task Ralco Ren Daul enjoyed immensely. Especially the women, he so liked watching them. Occasionally he'd mess with one. A quick pawing, fumbling, or maybe something more substantial when the master wasn't around.

He'd had most the girls, a few of the boys too. The slaves were terrified of Ralco. A black look from him could have them wetting themselves. That control over their fear was the best part.

As a youngster, the huge ungainly youth had been thrown out of the Daul tribe. Ralco didn't fit in. A clumsy spiteful giant, he'd killed a man in a brawl. They'd taken his tongue for that and dragged him out into the desert, naked, staked and starved—left as food for ants, flies and hyenas.

But Ralco hadn't died. He'd bitten through the cord, half strangling himself in the process, and stumbled back through the desert, surviving on cactus and carrion, until he reached the perpetrators.

They were playing dice that day, those five men charged with Ralco's punishment. He'd caught up with them at dusk, torn the face clean off the first man. The others weren't so lucky.

After that he'd been hunted down like a rabid wolf. Barakani, the new Lord of the Desert had recently united the tribes. The hunting parties were more organized.

Ralco was cornered in the hills south of Agmandeur, a city on the edge of the known desert. It had been Dracal who saved him that day. His master knew Barakani's huntsmen and paid them off.

Ralco Ren Daul had paid his master back many times over since then. Fiercely loyal, even Dracal's score of soldiers daren't mess with him.

Ralco was watching one of the girls climbing up the hill, her shift was torn, the dark sleek skin glistening. He liked this one. Jarmei, taken from a boat three weeks ago. Yamondon. Tall. Athletic.

The girl saw him standing there and cast her eyes down at her feet. Ralco smiled at the fear on her face, strolled over to where she struggled with the heavy water pitcher balanced on her right shoulder.

He'd knock that off and then punish her for carelessness. An enjoyable leisurely punishment to help pass the time during a monotonous morning.

But Ralco paused, hearing distant noises, and looking up saw a horse and rider approaching camp at speed. Two soldiers were already riding out to greet the newcomer, and Ralco guessed this must be his master returning from the city.

But where were his men, the slaves he'd bought? Dracal never returned alone. Something had happened. Ralco forgot the girl and strode down to the camp to await the cloud of dust approaching up the track.

*****

Dracal rode in at speed, the two soldiers flanking him. He dismounted, saw the giant mute, Ren Daul walking down the hill. He motioned Ren over and told the soldiers to start breaking camp.

"We ride south," Dracal announced briskly. Some of the soldiers looked askance, but Ralco, standing in their midst folded his massive arms and smiled. They kept their peace. Twenty paid fighters—his private army. Purchased from slimy Selimo, Dracal's contact in the city. Loyal to his coin, unlike Ralco who would die for him and smile while doing so.

The leader, Stron, a lean, hook-nosed brawler contracted from Syrannos approached. He glanced sideways at Ralco who stood grinning with those massive arms still folded. They didn't like Ralco Ren, these mercenaries.

"Where to?" Stron asked.

"Where I say," Dracal said. "We ride until I decide we've ridden enough."

"Why?" Stron stood his ground, and close by some of his men had hesitated at their tasks. Dracal needed patience. He'd happily stab this man in the throat, or have Ralco tear his ears off. But Stron had the full support of his men. Dracal needed them more than ever. Once free of this current predicament he'd acquire more fighters, and do away with this lot.

"I pay you for protection not to ask questions."

"The south holds nothing but desert," Stron said. "Are you in trouble, Master Dracal?" Ralco walked closer but Dracal bid him relax.

"A development in the city," he shrugged as though it were nothing of import. "An unfortunate incident—a careless murder has left the Sultan in a rare foul mood. His Guard will soon be searching all camps in the vicinity of Sedinadola for the perpetrators. We are merely being cautious. You know how heavy-handed those Crimson get."

"They don't usually give a shit unless it's one of their own," Stron said, and laughed. "Did you kill one of the Sultan's Elite, Dracal?"

A flash of irritation washed over him, and before he could stop himself Dracal had plunged his dagger into Stron's neck. The man slumped forward, fell to his knees and then collapsed, blood soaking the sandy ground.

The other mercenaries were all looking his way. Ralco circled slowly, arms out, ready for action. "I'm doubling your pay once we're back in business," Dracal said. They didn't move. But neither did Ralco.

"Stron was hasty—I'd have explained in more detail given the chance."

"How much gold?" The nearest called out. Rylen, a sly northerner. Snake Eyes, they called him. Outlawed up there.

"Lots," Dracal said. "You know how rich I am. Stay with me, we'll let this incident boil over. A few weeks and the Sultan will have forgotten, and Sedinadola will be begging for its favorite slaver. You'll see. They'll pay generously and you'll get a triple share. Just stick around."

"But Stron was right—the Elite were involved?"

"Yes," Dracal said. "And they can be obnoxious bastards at the best of times. We ride south and lie low. Get the camp struck and those fucking slaves ready for a journey. I'm done talking, Rylen."

Dracal turned away, confident he'd won them over. Minutes later his gamble paid off and the mercenaries started striking tents, dismantling and loading up the camels. A camp this size would take hours before they could leave. Dracal hoped they had hours, and that the Crimson weren't already riding his way.

Another gamble—such was life.

***

Captain Ralance Jago of the Sultan Elite's Second Wing stood stock still as his General addressed him in short sharp manner. He was tense and angry, hostile at being accosted in such a way. Unlike Gortansez, Jago was related to the Royal Household, albeit distantly—a bastard second cousin. But all the same.

"Your troop, Ralance—you are responsible." Jago knew that General Gortansez had had to explain to the Vizier Baizeefa and the Sultan's favorite son exactly what had transpired down at the docks last night.

The interview had not gone well and Gortansez saw fit to unleash his rage on the duty officer.

"And still no news?"

"We've cordoned the entire city, Sir," Jago said. "We have over a hundred suspects in for questioning. We will get those responsible. It's only a matter of time."

"There is no time!" Gortansez loomed over him, a huge man with bristling moustache and immaculate garb. He'd risen through the ranks, had the general. Had no time for sliders like Jago. Rich boys whose fathers had paid for their privilege of rank. Toy soldiers, Gortansez called them. Jago had heard him say it.

Jago didn't see it that way. He was dutiful and loyal. What had happened last night had left a stain on his honor, despite him being in the occupied at the other end of the city. The tenants of his favorite opium den would vouch for that. But Jago decided it best not to mention that. Gortansez had to rage at someone. Might as well be him.

"You and I are summoned to appear before the Sultan this evening," Gortansez said, his finger poking into Jago's chest.

Jago stiffened, more at the words spoken than the poke. *The Sultan.* He suddenly felt giddy. Not the best news he'd heard.

Hours later he stood stiffly beside his superior as the vizier inspected them and nodded them to enter. Baizeefa was a rake-thin individual with viper eyes, wispy beard and acid tongue. The Sultan's Hangman they called him, and for good reason. Feared and hated, Baizeefa had been responsible for the execution of hundreds in his career.

"On your bellies," Baizeefa snapped as they entered the golden haze that was the Sultan's private reception. A wide spacious hall comprising, gilded tables draped in foreign rugs and furs, lanterns, and candles, glinting, priceless jewel-encrusted throws and carpets— they were crawling on one now—hounds lolling and the Sultan's jester sticking his tongue out.

There were four naked women lying around a partly-clad fat man. The Sultan's favorite son, and heir, Samadin was renowned for his decadent tastes.

The Sultan's lazy voice addressed them from somewhere behind tapestries and screens. "Who is responsible for yesterday's abomination?" The voice lacked interest despite the words.

"Speak, before I have your tongues pulled out!" Baizeefa again.

"Eminence, we are still looking for the assassins," Gortansez said. "Your city is in lockdown; the foreign sailors and their captains have all been interrogated and found wanting. It now looks as though the slaver Dracal was involved. The last man questioned mentioned his name before we cut off his hands and feet and tossed him to the sharks."

"Dracal—you certain of this?" Another voice. Jago recognized Selimo's oily tones. A merchant rumored to be a spy, and another favorite of the Sultan.

"My Lord—yes," Gortansez said. "He had been there purchasing merchandise with his men."

"The men you butchered this morning, before even bothering to question them," the vizier almost spat on Jago, he was leaning so close.

"Well, that's most unfortunate." The sultan sounded bored. "An atrocity inside our city must be dealt with, General. We hold you personally responsible. You may leave us."

Jago saw the Vizier nod stiffly and he and the general shuffled back out the door on their bellies. The two soldiers followed suit. Once outside in the lobby, Jago clambered to his feet and dusted down his uniform. There were no other Crimson around. Word of this shouldn't leave the palace.

Moments later he saw Gortansez pacing briskly to the outer doors, but Jago lingered for a moment. Then turned, hearing a soft tread behind him, the Sultan's son Samadin stood there.

He made to kneel but Samadin placed a note in his hands. "Your orders, General," the Sultan's son had a nasally sickly voice and an unsavory smell lingered around his royal person.

General?

Jago bowed, accepted the note and bowed again. Hiding his sudden excitement. Then he withdrew and walked briskly to catch up his leader. Before joining him, Jago stopped at a corner, broke the seal and read the note's content. Two words.

Kill Gortansez.

Ralance Jago smiled secretly, his bastard cousin had come in handy.

Later that night he stole inside Gortansez' study and stabbed him in the heart. A common thug was held accountable. A man the newly promoted General had had placed in the vicinity, and executed soon after.

Word was out that Gortansez had failed and his replacement would make short work of the tasks ahead.

Another note arrived by courier that evening as General Ralance Jago settled comfortably into his new spacious quarters. Again, from Samadin.

Bring me Dracal's head. Do not fail else I'll have yours.

Ralance Jago felt the day's brief joy evaporate. *You're only as good as your last job.*

***

Ta-Kai watched the long column of riders filing south into the heat haze. Beyond them, huge dusty peaks of sand ranged left to right far as the eye could see. *The High Dunes* were rumored impassible. She shifted, squeezed and morphed into a heron, reaching out with her long gray wings and lifting, catching the breeze, gliding down and over to the distant riders. A camp on the move.

She flew close, but not near enough to receive a probing arrow. They were skirting *The High Dunes*, following a stony dry riverbed south west to a distant ridge, and a faint glint of water. Dracal's next campsite.

Satisfied with her reconnaissance, Ta-Kai circled and glided back north to where her hired carriage and the young woman inside waited for the next move.

She had done well, but had to report back these latest events. She waited till nightfall, glanced in on Nalissa's sleeping face, told her guards they'd be selling the carriage in the morning and purchasing camels for a long ride south.

The men hadn't quibbled; they all dreaded her.

This time she chose a hawk, swift and strong, soaring up into the thermals, the cold clean air exhilarating her and filling her with joy. *A long flight.* But not for her. She settled on his tower as morning lit that cold northern city.

As she'd expected he was waiting by the window. She became a woman again, climbed through the opened window and Lord Caswallon welcomed her inside.

"The girl?' His voice was strong, a man with real power and the only mortal she respected. A canny, careful man. Lord Caswallon.

"Safe," the Aikashi accepted the meal he'd arranged for her, and drank the offered wine.

"And my enemy?"

"Hasn't shown his hand—but he will."

"You sound confident," Caswallon said. "How so?"

"Because I mean to visit him personally and explain what's about to happen to his darling daughter."

Part Two
The Lynx

Chapter 13 | Infiltrators

"I don't want to be here," Coly muttered beside him, and Hagan grumbled something inaudible. Ahead, the gates loomed, tall ornate and heavily guarded by everyone's favorites. The Crimson Elite. The sultan's private army.

Corin had had dealings with this lot before. A set-to in an alley. Close call. Another woman had helped him that day, and old friend and a lover. Betrayed and murdered in that massacre, he alone had survived. It was part of the reason why Corin left the Regiment, though there were other factors involved.

"Walk slowly," Corin said. "We belong here." They were dressed in suitable desert garb, hardly discernable from the twenty or so other tribesmen mooching toward the gates, or dragging spitting camels. One or two wealthy types cantered past with horses, heads high as they whipped and lashed anyone in their way.

"Are they as dangerous as their reputation?" Hagan asked Corin; they were approaching the gates, so talking in whispers.

"Overrated in my opinion," Corin said. "But still dangerous, and treacherous murdering bastards to boot. They were our allies against the rebel tribes, though we did their dirty work."

"Aye, so I heard," Hagan said.

"Then the sultan patched it up with the rebel lord Barakani, and we were no longer needed—or welcome. The Crimson were charged with expelling mercenaries and ex-regiment lads from Permio's cities. They were ruthless," Corin said. "Few northerners dared stay in Syrannos, none in this city."

"That's comforting," pony-tail Coly said, affecting a limp as they approached the gates.

These loomed like a statement, gilded on hinges and frames, great oak monsters twelve feet high with more gold embossed on ribbing and studs. The barbican's crenulations showed above, and walls either side were comprised of sandstone, with archers' slots showing every ten feet. There were guards up there in crimson cloaks, pacing back and forth. Occasionally one would look down and spit on the desert folk below.

"Nice," Coly said. "I suspect they'll be after us in Cappel soon enough, no safe havens left."

Corin shrugged, looked about. Time to get sharp. "The sultan doesn't like Cappel Cormac, neither do his Crimson. Those posted back east are usually on probation for poor service and desperate to get home. Cappel's too dirty and dangerous for them. Unpredictable. People in that city are so poor they don't care."

Corin saw spearmen nudging and pushing at men as they hustled to get inside the city. Habitually he reached behind his shoulder and remembered Clouter was propped against his tent back in their makeshift camp. Instead he carried a large curved dagger and two throwing knives hidden up his sleeves.

He wasn't sure if weapons were allowed inside the city, but sometimes you had to take chances. Corin looked up at the walls where high gonfalons and pennants fluttered and flapped. Beneath these was a grisly sight. Six severed heads spiked on poles, the carrion circling above.

The guards looked resplendent in their famous long red cloaks, the gilded crimson-plumed helms, and fine meshed chain mail. They wore black boots laced with silver thread, and golden belts where scimitars, crossbows and knives clattered. Even the spears they hefted had gold lace attached.

Corin curled a lip—*Tossers.*

The right gate was open enough for men to squeeze through one at a time. The left remained shut. Corin, Hagan and Coly waited until a noisy knot of grubby goat herders approached. *This is our chance.*

"Go for it!" Corin hissed, and the three forced their way inside the haphazard cluster of goat herds, receiving blows and cusses but pushing through until they were surrounded by scrambling goats, jingling bells, and stinking nomads. *Perfect disguise.* The guards waved that company through without a second glance; the nearest had his nose covered by a crimson handkerchief.

Once free of barbican and walls, Corin shuffled away from the crowd and stopped to take stock. What he saw was a city very different from Cappel Cormac. For starters it was clean. No beggars, no stray mangy dogs, and no barefoot half-starved children running about.

The streets were freshly scrubbed from night soil and animal shit, and Corin saw long runnels hemming the main entrance, gutters where filthy water and detritus was allowed to find drain holes in the walls and exit the city.

The street ahead was a twisted knife, working up and around, the sandstone buildings leaning over. A circle within a circle. They followed the road up and the city rose beside them.

Carts clattered, men cursed; Corin saw women talking quietly in a corner. Goats, camels, the odd aloof rider on horse cantering past. A squad of Crimson Guard shouting and crunching the cobbles, forcing everyone off the street.

The three infiltrators huddled in the door of a building. Start at the top and work down—that had been Hagan's idea. Corin didn't have a better one. There would be more guards up there but they'd get a good view of the city and should spot the slave quarters, markets, or wherever these bastards conducted their filthy affairs. Corin had a low opinion of the slave trade—banned for thousand years in the north, but thriving as always down here.

The Crimson vanished around a corner. Corin nodded at the others and they stepped out, recommenced their climb toward the upper city. They passed gardens, walls trailing vine, jasmine, and clematis. Corin saw fountains, palms shading ornate benches, the occasional scholar or priest at study in the shade.

It was hot, but a sea breeze reached them this far up, and off to the right Corin glimpsed a thin line of blue. *The ocean.* He felt a pang of homesickness thinking of long lost Finnehalle, his village so far away in distance and time. Another life—*Will I ever return?*

They reached an arch, walked beneath it. Two guards sat dicing. Neither looked their way; the main thoroughfare would always be busy at this hour, which was why they had chosen it. Half an hour, and they were sweating despite the helpful breeze. Corin stopped, glanced through a gap in houses and saw the desert far below.

He followed its sandy haze until he glanced water miles away. A puddle it seemed, with tents like tiny triangles surrounding it. No doubt some trader's desert camp. Corin looked the other way, saw the ocean, the Silver Strand, the docks and harbor closer below him.

"We're near the top—what now?" Hagan said, face concealed beneath his djellaba.

"We find someone, ask a few questions," Corin said, fingering his curved knife and wishing he had Clouter in reach. They'd be lucky to vacate this place without a ruckus.

"That simple?" Hagan hinted a half grin. "Don't know why I bothered asking."

"What's that?" Coly said, and Corin heard a young voice crying out in sudden pain and fear. A sob, then plaintive yell, sound of a blow. Corin frowned, took three steps forward. A young lad by the sound of it.

Corin, stop—it's not our affair," Hagan hissed behind him. Corin kept walking. Sometimes you had to get involved. He turned a corner, saw the domed temple in full majestic glory ahead.

Much nearer—and smaller—were two figures, shouting. A man looming over a boy, a switch in his fist, and the boy ducking as he was struck relentlessly.

Corin picked up his pace, saw the blood on the boy's face and legs. *Poor little bugger.* Some guttersnipe, no doubt—and beggars not tolerated in this town.

Boy and man saw his approach. The lad's eyes were big with surprise; the man looked angry.

"Who are you?" They were the only words he got out before Corin's palm crunched under his nose and launched him backwards. He lay, a silent crumple. The boy looked at the mess and then scarpered.

"Hey!" Corin hissed, knelt down, pilfered the unconscious man's purse, and lifted a useful looking dagger. He stowed that one in his belt. *You can never have enough sharp things in this life.*

He turned, saw Hagan and Coly looking anxious behind him. Corin waved them back and hissed at the boy again, now hovering at a corner.

Hey, Matey," Corin managed a lopsided grin. The lad was poised like a deer before flight. Corin suspected he hadn't experienced kindness before. "I've some copper coins," he opened the stolen purse and rolled a large coin other to the lad, who kneeled and scooped it up with deft little fingers.

"I'll part with silver for information," he smiled again, and the boy stepped backwards. Maybe smiling was a bad idea.

Corin!" Hagan's urgent hiss behind.

"What information?" The boy's accent was thick with the desert. Corin wondered how he came to be here.

"Tell me where the slave quarters are—where their purchased and sold."

"Not here," the boy said, and then jumped as the man at Corin's feet rose to his knees and reached for his missing knife. Corin kicked him in the face and stamped hard on his neck. Bones crunched.

"Don't think he'll trouble you again," Corin said.

The boy smiled savagely. "That's good," He said. "He was a cunt."

Corin raised an eyebrow. "So, help me here." He walked across and leaned over the walls, glancing out casually, the boy watched him with wary eyes.

"They your friends?" The lad pointed to Hagan and Coly still standing with clenched fists close by.

"Companions. We're goat herders."

"More likely goat fuckers," the boy laughed. "You're northern mercenaries."

"How can you tell?" Corin was shocked. This lad was sharper than he'd expected.

"You might as well wear badges with your country's name," the boy said. "If the Crimson weren't so up themselves they'd have nabbed you by now."

"What's your name?" Corin said.

"Dully."

"Well Master Dully, we're on important business and need to get moving. But you can help us—more silver." He risked the smile again. This time the boy nodded. He walked over to the dead man and spat on his robe.

"Name was Kialla," Dully said. "A retainer from the House of Selimo. He's the man you need to find, conducts business with the slavers for the sultan."

"Good to know, boy," Hagan had approached and loomed over the lad. Dully glared up at him, no fear in that young face. Corin guessed he was around fourteen, maybe younger. Sharp as freshly honed steel.

"Where do we find this Selimo?" Corin asked, and then noticed Coly waving his arms about. "What?"

"Soldiers coming—half a dozen."

"How far?" Hagan said.

"Five minutes." Coly looked ready to run.

Corin could hear the crunch of steel shod boots on stone somewhere below, and getting nearer.

"Wait here," Corin bid the boy stay put as he and Hagan each grabbed a leg and dragged the deceased Kialla into a shady corner, a convenient magnolia bush providing ample cover.

Coly jumped alongside, and Corin beckoned at Dully to join them. The boy hesitated, looked down the street and shrugged. He joined them, a grin splitting his face.

"You'll be dead by nightfall," Dully told them.

"Thanks for the vote of confidence," Coly said.

"That may be," Corin said to the boy as the other men crouched low. "Nature of our work." The soldiers were appearing around the corner. They waited, two, three minutes. The guards passed, scarce yards from their hideout. Their eyes were focused on the temple so they didn't notice the thin trail of blood staining the cobbles beneath their fancy boots, though one fellow swatted a fly from his face.

Corin smiled—he'd counted on that.

"No man can out live his destiny," he told the boy and saw Hagan rolling his eyes. "We three are about saving someone. An important and risky business, and a lot depends on us succeeding. You can help, Dully."

"I'd sooner not hang," Dully said, and shrugged again as Corin dropped a stolen silver piece in his grubby nubbins.

"Selimo?" Corin asked, slipping another coin free. Something brushed past his face and Corin saw a black bird settle on a branch. The thing watched him with coaly black eyes. The sight made him shiver, a strange sense of dread creeping up his spine. *Trust your instinct.* The bird took wing and vanished.

"His mansion is nearby," Dully said. He hadn't noticed the bird, neither by their looks had his friends. "Backs on to the Sultan's Royal Gardens. Selimo's allowed private access by grace of his master."

"This Selimo must be important," Corin said. Hagan nudged him and he nodded. This was taking too long. "So where can we find him?"

"Selimo takes smoke and ease in the gardens around lunchtime," Dully said. "That's about now—so most likes where he'll be. But you won't get inside the gardens with your heads attached."

"We're fond of our heads," Corin said, nodding sagely.

"Then turn back and flee while you can," Dully said. "Linger and the Crimson will find you, linger longer and it's curfew—that's execution if you're caught on the street, or maiming if they're feeling gentle."

"We've a job to do, Dully," Corin smiled. "Needs must. Our profession."

"Dying?" The boy blinked at him. "Short career."

"Staying alive in tricky circumstances," Corin corrected. "We're a kind of special hit team. Guerilla squad." Dully seemed impressed by that. "So where are these Royal Gardens?"

"Behind that temple," Dully said, scratching an ear. "Beyond them is the sultan's palace."

Corin tossed the purse in the dirt. Dully snatched it with practiced ease. "Take care young fella—and thanks." Corin winked at the boy and stood up, the street was empty again.

Hagan slapped the boy's head affectionately and Dully punched him in the leg.

"Hang to those silly heads," the boy said then vanished behind the magnolia tree. A survivor with a story Corin would never know.

"Tough little bugger," Coly said, glancing back at the bushes.

"Reminds me of my younger self," Hagan said.

"Now for the fun part," Corin said and jumped back onto the road, the midday sun hitting him like a hammer. The temple loomed close, white and gold and hugely grotesque, blinding in the sun, the road curving to its left. Beyond that a hint of green. The gardens. Their destination.

Getting in would be tricky. Getting out alive considerably harder. Corin would fret on that later. Focus on one step at a time. *Best foot forward…*

***

Selimo leaned back in the chair as he inhaled the smoke from his hookah. A hot day, but not unpleasantly so—especially in the Royal Gardens where shade was plentiful and only beauty tolerated. Slaves were never seen here, though they worked constantly to shape shrubs, cut around paths, plant trees, move trees no longer required. But never visible to the gentle folk taking their ease. Being spotted meant a flogging, or worse.

The gardens were reserved for the sultan and his favorite people. A small, privileged group of citizens that Selimo had worked hard to join. Very hard. He was born poor.

That had made him tenacious, hungry for wealth. And when he acquired enough of that, even hungrier for power. *Power was the key.*

It got things done. Selimo guessed he was number three in this city, perhaps four—Vizier Baizeefa the Administrator and his rival, had a big following. But only Prince Samadin and the Sultan himself were stationed above Selimo.

He had achieved the impossible, and chose these quiet reflections in the gardens to remind himself, preen his feathers. Selimo wasn't even Permian but had fled the jungle tribes of Golt seeking work in the city. He was clever and ruthless, good with a knife. He'd murdered, stolen, and bribed, even whored his body as a young man—anything to clamber up the greasy pole.

Opulent and powerful, he owned a mansion that backed onto the sultan's, had thirty-five retainers and a squad of one dozen Elite Crimson Guard reserved for his own private uses, courtesy of the Sultan.

And yet he wasn't happy. A practiced schemer and conniver, Selimo had jumped on the opportunity to renew communications with the tyrant in the north. The High King, or *Crystal King* as he was sometimes called, for reasons beyond Selimo's knowledge. That distant ruler was rumor, a mythical figure, but his Lord Counselor and Iron Hand was terrifyingly real. Word was, this Caswallon was also a sorcerer. Few men frightened Selimo, he was one.

Caswallon had sent much needed troops south during the war with the rebel tribes, and conveniently called them back after the truce, so the Crimson Elite could claim that work as their own. There was long-standing correspondence between Sedinadola and that northern city. A great deal of secrecy. The sultan had needed a man to journey north and represent his eminence. A discreet shrewd individual. Selimo fitted glove perfect for the task.

He'd been received in that drafty tower, the lone fire blazing and solitary window hinting the dismal wet-cold city, so very far below. A miserable visit, and a dangerous one. Caswallon got inside a man.

Those dark probing eyes... There were things he'd found out about Selimo, certain details the sultan need not know. And wouldn't know—unless Selimo failed his new master in the north.

Hooked and caught.

The *Aikashi* had been a surprise, and not a pleasant one. The letter had arrived a couple of weeks back.

> *There's a man I need to break, mold and remodel.*
> *Sending an agent with details. An Aikashi.*
> *Do not cross her!*
> *Expect your full support.*
> *C.*

That was more than sufficient to put his back up. And then *she*—the aforementioned agent—had paid him that visit, and worse the second visit last week. The *Aikashi*—Caswallon's conjured Killer: The Lynx. A shapeshifter and remnant of an extinct race. Dragged screaming from the void by unspeakable sorcery.

Fortunately, Selimo was clever enough to appease both his masters. He'd informed Caswallon via pigeon of his last meeting with the Lynx. Mentioned Dracal, and details about the slaver which should satisfy. *Should...*

Enough! Selimo puffed at the hemp. *I worry for no reason. All is in hand.*

Selimo managed a smile; the smoke always made him feel better. He'd head back to the villa soon for a scented bath, a girl or two rubbing him down and satisfying his other needs. Life was good for the privileged few in Sedinadola.

A rustle in the bushes close by. A bird perhaps? Selimo sucked at the pipe and then froze, the sharp prick of a dagger prodding his throat.

A face loomed close. A hard face that didn't suit the djellaba covering it. A second face appeared closer, scarred, miserable, long, and easily recognizable as a despised northerner. Had Caswallon sent people to kill him? Selimo felt certain that wasn't the case. Caswallon had the Lynx, so why bother with amateurs. *But who then...?*

"My name's Corin," the one with the scarred face said. The other, a nasty looking individual with pale gray eyes, placed a finger on his lips and produced a knife. He grabbed Selimo's hand and pricked the blade under a fingernail.

"To ensure you're paying attention," that one said. Selimo remained stock still. Three men. The third hidden behind him holding the blade to his throat.

"Here's the thing," the one called Corin said. "I'm seeking someone, and have good reason to believe you know where she is."

He leaned forward, the long face hovering close and stinking of garlic. Blue/gray eyes the color of northern seas. Selimo gulped.

"Think he wants to speak," the voice came from the hidden one behind him. The scarred one, Corin, nodded and the knife was withdrawn from his throat. Selimo took a long slow, very careful breath.

"I think this is a mistake—" He gasped as the nail was prized deftly from his index finger. Pop, slice. Selimo looked down in horror at the blood welling and sudden sharp pain. Gray Eyes had the knife under his middle finger now.

"No. That was a mistake," Gray Eyes winked at him.

"We haven't got all day, Hagan—maybe just cut his fucking hands off. You brought the hatchet?" Scarface Corin again.

"I've got it here," the one he couldn't see.

"Wait!" Selimo almost sobbed the word out. *Who are these people?* "I will assist as I can, but I don't think—"

"Name Silon mean anything."

Selimo had an ice-cold feeling in his belly. *Silon.* These were his people. He nodded quickly. "I've heard it mentioned. A merchant from Raleen?"

"Currently looking for his daughter," Corin said. "Stolen—feared sold in the slave markets of this city."

Selimo was thinking fast. *So, these were Silon's men, but did they know about Caswallon and the Lynx? Unlikely.* He took a gamble.

"New slaves are managed in the camps south of the city," he said, forcing confidence into his words. The hour was approaching afternoon. The Guard should be changing soon and one or two usually stopped by to check the gardens. *Keep your cool, hold them here.* "Specifically, one—the slaver's name is Dracal. He collects new meat at the docks and…" Selimo regretted his choice of words as Hagan stabbed at his finger, a second nail ripping free.

"Have a care, mate," the one behind him again. "My pals don't approve of slime like you." Selimo heard distant voices, people approaching. He prayed to Telcanna that was the guards.

"Dracal will have the girl if she was brought here." Boots coming this way through the pathways. The imposters stood back. Glanced around sharply.

"Where's his camp?" Scarface Corin said, but the first soldier emerged through the bushes and froze.

"Imposters—seize them!" Selimo yelled before the knife tore into his throat, and blood and pain choked him.

Shouts, steel clashing, the bright sunshine all faded, crinkled and fell apart like parchment tossed in a fire. His plans, his world—gone. And for what? Selimo was slipping down into void, a tossed stone vanishing in a well. Blackness and pain reached up and pulled him down gagging through the earth.

Chapter 14 | Departure Time

"Whoops…" Hagan said wiping his knife on Selimo's robe and then stowing it away. Corin felt suddenly older, weary, and downright miserable.

"He could have told us more," he said, glancing over to where the seven warriors stood, mouths gaping, their polished armor gleaming in the sun.

A moments calm reflection before the carnage.

"The shithead hollered, so I sliced him," Hagan explained, slipping his sword into a fist. Corin wished he had Clouter. Three knives wouldn't cover it. A whole rack would be insufficient.

More Elite were pushing through the first seven. At last someone important arrived. A tall captain, or officer of sorts. "So," he said. "The imposters from the other night have returned. Foolish." His men looked at him.

"What?" Corin said. "We were just out for a stroll, saw this poor fellow. He's wasn't feeling well, so Hagan here put him out of his misery."

"They've murdered Selimo," a soldier said to his leader. The leader took stock of the corpse and nodded slowly.

"These are the same brigands, for sure. Mad dogs." He turned to Corin and the others. "Lay down your steel so we can arrest you and drag you in chains before the vizier for ritual dismemberment and castration."

"Not today thank you," Corin said.

"I'd sooner pass," this from Hagan.

"Yeah, think we'll wait for a better offer," Coly added from behind.

"Been a nice little visit," Hagan coughed. Corin looked down. Selimo's blood was watering the roses. Strange how plans go awry so quickly.

There must have been at least twenty red-cloaked guards smoldering in the gardens. Glittering armor, and long cloaks, spears and swords. No archers in view. They were hesitant—uncertain how to proceed. Even the captain seemed taken back by their response. He was about to say something when Corin's tossed dagger found his chest.

The officer looked down in disbelief, muttered something incoherent and fell to his knees, his soldiers leaning over him in stunned silence. He looked across at Corin for the briefest moment, and then pitched faced first into a thorn shrub.

"Think we'd better leave now," Hagan said.

"Run!" Corin yelled, as the first spear flew past his head. They were on them, angry as wasps in late summer. Another spear flying past, yells, a rush of steel-shod feet. Corin ran one way, his comrades legged it in other directions. He heard Coly shout something, and a loud ripping crash followed by curses hinted Hagan had impacted some bushes. No time to worry about those two.

Let's just get through this morning with our heads on. He ran. Jumped over benches, crashed through fronds and wagging palms, cut left and right, voices yelling close behind. Dived through a tunnel of bush, crawled on, and then rolled and found his feet by the garden walls.

Leaping up, Corin found a hand hold, swung his tired bones up and rolled over, dropping like a potato sack on the cobbles of a side street. Ahead, the temple loomed like a giant white eggshell, traced with gold. Gaudy, but Corin lacked the recreation for a proper appraisal.

Yells across the wall, sound of boots and hands scrambling. A head appeared and then vanished after Corin's second knife flew.

He sprinted down the cobbled lane and vaulted over a low wall crashing into another garden, this one private, some wealthy merchant perhaps? He lay low in a bush, got his wind back. Boots rushing past, a glint of steel. More shouts, and now new voices coming from further off. *Whole damn city's hunting for us.*

The voices trailed off again. Corin clambered out the bush and had a look around. Close by on a trellis a bird preened its wings. A raven; it watched him with indifference.

Alright for you. Corin could use a pair of wings today. *Here we go.* No plan. The last one hadn't worked out that well. *Just stay alive, and keep moving.*

He left that spacious yard, the fountains tinkling behind him, the eyeless statues draped in ivy, the wide pool carpeted with water lilies.

He found a gate, made for it and then crashed into someone. A scream, which he managed to stifle by covering her mouth with a hand. A youngish girl, plainly clad in white tunic and sandals. She looked terrified, her dark skin sheening with sweat.

"Not going to hurt you," Corin whispered in her ear. "Having a rough day," he explained. "Need to leave this city soonest."

The girl's eyes were huge with panic. "I'm not going to hurt you," Corin repeated. "Please don't scream." Carefully he withdrew his calloused hand from her mouth. She stood there like a deer trapped by torchlight, frozen, on the edge of flight.

"What's your name?" Corin whispered.

"Slaves are seldom given names," she said, her eyes everywhere as if she expected company.

"You are a slave?" She nodded and then looked at him as though he were stupid. "Oh, well, we don't allow slaves where I come from," Corin told her."

"I'm a Vendeli," she said, her eyes still scanning the gardens. "The Yamondons raided my village, took us to the coast and sold us to Permian slavers."

And he thought he'd had a rough childhood. Corin was aware he needed to get moving. But where? He took a chance.

"Will you help me escape? Maybe know somewhere I can hideout until dark?"

Corin saw her expression and rested his hand on her shoulder. He smiled. "I'm sorry—not your problem, and I don't want to get you in trouble."

"They'd feed me to the dogs," she said.

"For helping me escape?"

"For taking too long to trim the bushes," she said. "The overseer..."

Fuck.

The sound of footsteps approaching. Corin turned and saw a large man standing there. He wore a wide leather belt with keys hanging, a short-curved sword, and a whip stowed alongside. His white robe had a broad red sash running from left shoulder to right hip. He was fat, his face fleshy, flustered, and furious.

Corin smiled at him. He grabbed the girl's arm before she could run. "Don't worry," Corin told her. "I'll handle this."

"It's the Master's overseer," the girl whispered.

"Who's the master?"

"Lord Selimo."

"Oh," Corin said and smiled at the overseer, who had unsheathed the evil looking curved sword and was preparing to attack.

Hesitation can prove fatal. "Think you're out of a job," Corin said as he walked calmly towards the man. The curved blade leaped toward his face. Corin twisted, knocked the steel aside with his forearm, and then jumped forward and jabbed his fingers up under the overseer's nose knocking him off his feet.

The sword clattered. Corin knelt, scooped up the blade. Nicely balanced. He swung it through his fingers. *Not bad at all.* The man opened his eyes just in time to see his own sword swinging for his neck.

"Guess you won't be feeding any more slaves to your dogs, Fat Boy." Corin watched the overseer's head roll into a shrubbery. He turned to the girl expecting she'd be horrified. Instead she was smiling.

"I know where we can hide," she told him. "Until nightfall, then my brother will help us. He knows a way out the guards never search."

"Your brother?"

"An escaped slave turned pick pocket, called Dully."

***

Hagan didn't like running. So, he chose to fight instead. They were confident. A mistake. The first careless spear thrust had him relieve the guard of his weapon, reversing it and imbedding the point in the spearman's belly.

Three had him cornered in the gardens, but Hagan had been beaten as a boy until he'd got a farmer to teach him the quarterstaff—the Morwellan peasants' preferred weapon. He'd been good. Same principles applied with a spear. Only spears were better because they've sharp bits on one end.

Hagan blocked a thrust, whirled his spear snapping the butt into one face, spun the weapon behind the legs of the next man, swiping him from his feet, reversed the weapon again, and stabbed down.

The third guard lunged low. Hagan spread his hands along the spear shaft, turned it sideways and rebuffed that blow, swinging around in a follow up move and rapping the guard on the back of his neck just below his helmet.

The man sprawled, Hagan stepped forward, stabbed down hard skewering that one. Then he finished off the one he'd hit with the blunt end, saw more coming and decided it time for departure. He took to the path, found a side cut, the wall, and vaulted over.

He trotted towards the shadow of a building shaded by palms, waited there as a squad of Crimson Guard filed past. Lying low to nightfall would be his best bet.

***

Coly ran full pelt for the main gate, tripped and sprawled with four guards crashing upon him, the fall surprising them as much as him. *Serendipitous.* Coly scrambled free of the mess and jumped up, started running again— judging by the shouts the guards were following close behind. Down through the corkscrew lanes, the upper city frowning upon him. Ducking as some helpful soul tossed night soil from a window.

Coly heard the guard yelling something obscene and smiled to himself. He must have caught that missile. A good runner, Coly got ahead, chanced a backwards glance. He'd lost sight of his pursuers. He saw a side cut, a cluttered alley with sheets and garments hanging from ropes spanning the narrow gap between buildings. He cut sideways, entered when he was sure no one was looking.

The city was still quiet up here, though below was busy, the bustle of marketplace and vendors reaching up to him.

He crouched low, trotted down the cut. A scraggy cat hissed and spat and him. Coly found another cut, even narrower, diverted that way. It stank in the alley, somewhere close a dog growled. Coly saw garments strung from a line. A shoddy robe, some kind of desert hat, discarded conveniently. He smiled again. The gods were kind today.

Coly threw the robe—still damp—over his shoulders, and removed his djellaba replacing it with the floppy hat, pulling the brim down to hide his features. He found a knotted stick in a gutter, covered in shit. Retrieved that, wiped some extra shit on his face—ample supply in the drain—and the robe, and hobbled out the alley like the cripple he resembled.

Coly made it to the gates where the Guard helpfully tossed him out amid yells curses and kicks.

"Stinking bastard," one spearman said.

"Thanks," Coly had replied under his breath and limped out of sight. Once free of those watching on the walls he tossed the stick, climbed out of his robe and sprinted for the nearest caravan train, the tents sprawled like pointy hats half a mile ahead.

***

Borgil squinted in the afternoon sun. Behind him, camels were biting each other, flies buzzed his face, the odd one bit, and nearby vendors were exchanging insults. *Shithole* didn't cover it. They should never have come here. It was Hagan's fault, him and the long-legged bastard with the big sword.

That sword was propped in a corner of one of their tents. Trusting? Not when Corin an Fol had threatened to cut out the liver of anyone who got near it, and then nail that organ to their head. Clearly hyperbole, but the way he'd said it saw the sword stayed put.

Not that Borgil cared overmuch for swords, he was more of an ax man. He could sweep, clean, hard and fast. Stocky and broad, his frame worked well with an ax. He had his stowed inside the loop on his belt. Like the kettle helm—he didn't see the need to remove it, even in this infernal heat.

Rejen and the other lads were playing dice, joking at a makeshift table they'd purloined. Their three tents were hidden amidst this vast camp of vendors, traders, cheese peddlers, goat shaggers and general villains.

Borgil didn't have standards, but if he had Permio would sit neatly at the bottom. And this camp would be the dregs of that barrel. Besides, something wasn't right—he could feel it. They'd been gone too long, those three.

He'd wandered through the camp earlier, squinting and blinking, cussing people—no problem as everyone did that here. The helmet got attention, not that Borgil cared about that. There was still the odd northerner working legally in this country, and few of those shifting eyes would trouble him with the ax swinging from his belt.

He'd reached a ridge, just past the camel corral, allowing wide views of the city walls. He counted nine tiny round objects stuck fast on poles; there were birds circling around them. Some had settled to feast. Fascinated, Borgil walked nearer. Three heads looked recent.

He wanted to make sure, but someone up there must have seen him as an arrow buzzed his way. Borgil got the hint, shunted back inside the maze of the caravan camp. He wasn't certain those were their heads, but chances were...

Borgil ambled back to his tent. He'd made his mind up and would be leaving soon. Not staying here another night. He stole a sly glance at the longsword still leaning against that table. He'd be dead by now. *I could take that.*

He turned when someone shuffled. A shadow by the flap. Thought he'd been alone in the tent. "Who's that?"

"Me," Borgil blinked seeing Coly sprawled on a chair, his boots rested on Borgil's supply chest. *Bastard's alive.* Borgil wasn't sure whether that was good news or not.

"Where the other two?"

Coly flicked his blonde pony-tail and yawned. "Be here soon I expect, had some trouble in the city."

"What kind of trouble?"

"The usual kind," Coly said. "Now piss off, and let me get some sleep."

Borgil left him and went outside where the others were still dicing. They ignored him so he wandered back to stare at the walls again.

"I'm not staying here," Borgil chewed his beard. "But I'll wait long enough to murder that long-legged bastard if he ain't dead already."

"You got a problem?" A vendor and his two guards were staring at Borgil.

"Trapped wind," Borgil said, and returned to his tent again.

***

Silon rolled from the bed and grabbed his knife as the shutter blew open. *No one there.* He tried his door, the corridor outside was empty. He glanced back at the windows again, the drapes flapping in the night breeze.

He picked up the cranked crossbow he always kept in his study, adjacent to his sleeping quarters. No sign of his retainer, or servants. He went to the kitchens. No one there either.

"They are all dead," the voice came from behind him.

Silon turned, fired the weapon and the bolt flew straight towards her head. It struck the wall and buried itself within. The woman had vanished.

Fingers sweating, Silon fumbled with a second bolt. "Where are you?" No answer. He saw the front doors to the villa were wide open, a body prone on the floor there. Tense with fear, Silon recognized his retainer, throat sliced open. He walked out into the gardens, saw three other corpses.

He walked quicker, feeling the rage and horror accompany his fear. 'What have you done with my daughter?" Silon shouted the words.

"Dracal the slaver has her." Her voice came from somewhere in the trees above. "Even now she's servicing his cock beneath the desert moon."

Silon glanced up, saw movement. A large owl watching him. He fired again and the owl lifted, effortlessly and faded off into the night.

Next morning Silon boarded a vessel at Port Sarfe, his destination Cappel and beyond. Corin an Fol had let him down. *Goes to show. Sometimes you have to do your own wet work in this life.*

Chapter 15 | Slave

Dracal's men were constructing the second camp when Ta-Kai rode in on the camel, the girl Nalissa chained to another beast she had tied behind her own. The giant mute saw her, wandered over.

"I've business with your master," she glared down coldly at the brute. "Go fetch him." The giant stared at her for a moment and then nodded curtly. Ta-Kai waited, glancing around at the makeshift camp being constructed.

She heard voices, then Dracal emerged hemmed by soldiers, mercenaries by their look. Northerners. Ta-Kai slid from the camel's back and stood waiting for their approach, her arms resting at her sides, a half smile on her face. The soldiers looked wary, Dracal afraid—tough man but out of his depths.

Dracal stopped several paces away, looked across at where the girl slumped like a sack of barley across the other camel's back. The mercenaries glanced that way too. No one spoke.

"So. Here we are." Ta-Kai folded her arms and allowed her smile broaden, revealing her teeth—freshly filed—just to get their reactions. They were alarmed, edgy. Unsure how to react. The one on the right shuffled his feet. Dracal looked at Nalissa again, a shape wrapped in a blanket. Prone, sleeping—or too exhausted to contribute to the day.

"Here we are," Ta-Kai said again, feigning a yawn. Still nothing. The men kept their hands away from their weapons, no doubt word had reached them about the incident at the harbor. They were cautious, expectant. "I have the girl," she said, hinting the other camel.

"I see her," Dracal's voice was raw, like he'd been up all night smoking. The slaver had rings under eyes, looked disheveled. "The prize you promised."

"Take her south into the deep desert and lie low."

"We're lying low here," one of the soldiers said. Ta-Kai ignored him.

"The Crimson Guard will find you here, like I did," she said. "Easy following a dry river bed." She turned brazenly showing them her back and walked calmly over to the second camel. She untethered her prisoner and heard an intake of breath as the men saw Nalissa's smoky locks spill from the blanket.

"Wake up, Sweetling—Your new master wants to inspect you," Ta-Kai dragged Nalissa from the camel's back and slapped her face. The girl spat at her and one of the soldiers laughed. Ta-Kai slapped her again, harder this time.

"I've a little trip to undertake," Ta-Kai said. "Be back in a few days—for payment," her eyes flicked across to Dracal, who was taking in Nalissa's beauty. He nodded, said nothing.

Nalissa blinked in the sunshine. Ta-Kai slapped her again, affectionately this time, as though she were her little sister. "Be good," she said, then turned to the slaver again. "Three days, maybe four. I'll return for my gold."

Dracal nodded again, looking like a man who'd reached a dead end with enemies closing in. She vaulted on the camel's back, flashed them all a magnificent smile and rode from the camp, the second animal clomping behind her own beast.

***

Dracal watched rider and camels fade into haze and dust, at last vanishing in a shimmer of distance. He turned to the girl standing there, wild-eyed, fists clenched. A beauty he wished he'd never seen. And what price would that creature demand? Didn't matter. He'd pay it somehow and the sorceress or whatever she was would leave him be. And hopefully the Crimson too, when word reached Selimo of this unfortunate state of affairs.

One of the soldiers coughed beside him. Dracal snapped his fingers. "Get those tents ready. We'll spend the night here then move south again."

"I like it here," Dracal turned to see Snake-Heart Rylen staring hard at his face. "Good position—and the lads are done with roaming. We're not breaking camp a second time, Slaver. We stay put."

Dracal didn't have time for this. "Fetch Ren Daul—would you? We'll discuss this further at nightfall." Rylen looked at him for a moment more, then nodded, and strolled off, the other men walking alongside. More trouble around the corner.

I'll deal with them later. Solve one problem at a time. That way a man kept his head above the waterline. He hoped the sharks would stay away.

Dracal looked at the girl again, appraising those long wavy locks, the proud face. The bruises only enhanced her beauty. Good figure, voluptuous, feisty. She would bring an excellent price once she was cleaned up. The girl stared at him, almost challenged him. Dracal like that. Made a change. Captive girls were usually so afraid. This one would take some breaking in.

Ralco Ren appeared by his side and for the first time the girl looked worried, shrinking back from the giant.

"This is Ralco Ren Daul," Dracal told the girl. "You obey his every signal very carefully. He can be quite sensitive when upset. Get

Ranysi," this last to the mute. "Tell her clean this one up." Dracal gave the girl a final appraisal, and walked off to see when the tents would be ready.

As he walked he formed an idea in his head, and for the first time that day he smiled. That girl was worth a small fortune. In Yamondo or Vendel, or any of those southern lands. A Raleenian beauty. She could be his ticket out of here. Rylen's mercenaries wanted to stay here—so let them. Dracal had other plans

He would leave before dawn, nice and silent, taking only Ralco and the Yamondon girl, Ranysi, who could keep an eye on his new prize. That way he'd avoid not only the Crimson Guard, but the Lynx woman as well. There was a cove twenty miles west of Sedinadola, frequented often by some old associates. A secret known only to those in his trade, ideal for the purpose.

The pirates of Crenna would pay handsomely for the Raleenian wench knowing they would double their money in the southlands. Dracal's smile widened. He was a nomad at heart. Time to move; he'd been in this part of the desert far too long. Grown stale, his wits needed honing again.

He found an outcrop with wide views over the camp and beyond. Dracal reached for the small pipe hidden in his pocket. He struck flint to tinder, lit up and leaned back against the sandstone. He closed his eyes and breathed in the heady smoke, finally relaxing after what had proved a very trying couple of days.

***

The giant terrified her, and the stench that lingered around his person left her gagging. He'd grabbed her once and shoved her down in the dirt, standing over, grinning like a diseased dog. Nalissa had closed her eyes at that point.

But she opened them again on hearing a woman's voice. The

giant had left. Instead a black-skinned woman surveyed her with hard critical eyes. She was tall and lean, muscular with a strong, beautiful face. Nalissa glared up at her.

"That...man..."

"Ralco Ren," the woman's accent was strange to her ears, husky and deep. She smiled briefly—a fierce ironic grin. "He has that effect on all of us." She reached down and pulled Nalissa to her feet with uncanny strength. "But I've a feeling he'll not lay a finger on you."

"How do you know?" Nalissa glanced about but there was no sign of Ralco."

"Call it a hunch," the woman said. "My people trust their hunches."

"You're...?"

"A Yamondon princess," the woman laughed bitterly. "Or rather I was, until the Vendel kidnapped me and sold me to that slime Selimo, and him to Dracal. No pretenses anymore. I've learned to please my masters, stay alive. You'll need to do the same."

"I'm not serving anyone," Nalissa said. "Especially in that way!"

"The black girl smiled patiently. "Then you will perish my dear. Come on—let's get you some food and clean the grime from your face. You're going to have to learn to please your master very soon. If you're clever, Dracal will keep you for himself. It's better than being passed around the camp like most of the girls here."

"I told you I'm not servicing that pig or anyone hereabouts." *The Lynx had deserted her.* Strange how she felt the sting of betrayal from a woman who she hated. The one who had caused her pain.

"I'm Ranysi," the young woman said ushering Nalissa into a large tent. Two girls were seated on rugs. Ranysi signaled and they stood up and left without a word. "Get some rest, I'll be back shortly to clean you up."

Nalissa watched Ranysi slip out of the tent. The fear came back when the other woman left her. What if that giant returned.

I'm Silon's daughter—not letting them win…

***

The craft beached on *The Silver Strand* a dozen miles west of Syrannos. Silon paid the smuggler handsomely and leaped ashore, the warm seawater soaking his garments as he waded onto the beach, a pack across his back, two throwing knives, a short sword, sling and stones, and enough dried beef for a three-day hike.

First up, lie low and wait for darkness. The moon was waning, and he'd make good progress ere sun up. The merchant reached the shelter of the dunes, unpackaged his pack and erected his makeshift cover, laying low, munching on dried meat, the sea birds crying, and waves crashing endlessly down on the shore.

He closed his eyes, allowing a half sleep relax his muscles. The next few days would test his every nerve.

***

Ralance Jago leaned back in his saddle and took stock of the scene ahead. A deserted campsite. The villain Dracal had fled with all his people, which was proof of his guilt. The general grunted as his soldiers rode through the camp looking for discards and signs, or hints of where they had gone.

It wasn't difficult to decipher. There was only one logical route. *South.* A dry river bed conveniently led that way, skirting the infamous *High Dunes,* a terrain rumored impassible. Flanking the dry river on its west was endless flat featureless desert—also rumored impassable. An empty world. Few ventured this way. Why would they?

Captain Coralion, his newly promoted second, rode up alongside the general. Sharp and eyed and ambitious, neat features, freshly clipped goatee. A soldier with prospects. "Clear marks from camel and horse, carts also. They have a day on us—no more."

"Good," Jago rubbed his stubble. "We shall have Dracal's head by dusk if things go to plan. Tell the men to remount. We'll follow the river bed."

"There's a small oasis several miles from here," Coralion said, rubbing sweat from his face. City lad, Coralion. Like Jago he was well connected and ambitious, and young enough not to pose an immediate risk to the newly promoted general. "That's where they'll be, Sir," Coralion flashed his confident smile.

Jago had sixty riders. That was all he could spare, as most were still stationed in and around the city in case there were others in league with the slaver. Jago couldn't understand Dracal's motives. The man was rich and successful, until now he'd had right of entry into the city even through curfew. Why throw all that away in some reckless venture? It didn't fit. There was something else going on here and General Ralance Jago was determined to be the man who unraveled the mystery.

***

Ta-Kai took her time, there was no need to rush. Guided her beasts up onto the high ridges of sand and watched as the crimson cloaked column of riders filed down from Dracal's recently abandoned camp close to the city. She counted sixty horsemen, and three officers stood out—all wore breastplates and helmets which glittered and announced their presence clearly even at this distance. Men were such fools.

She thought of Dracal, his mercenaries. Stupid and petty. How had this race outwitted her own? Ta-Kai felt that ancient rage, the old grudge rising like a bile worm in her belly. *Her people gone forever, and these shallow creatures the victors.* She would have to kill again soon. The need was on her.

She lay low throughout that day; the relentless desert sun bothered her fair skin—whichever form she took. Hers were a people more comfortable in darkness.

The riders past beneath her, a clatter of hoof on stone, voices, steel and leather clonking, the sun dazzling off their polished steel.

She waited until they were out of sight and then guided her beasts back down to the dry river bed. She needed to contact Selimo, report the job done. But there was no rush. She returned to the caravan camp where they'd sold the carriage. She hired a tent, slept for a time, until dusk turned the desert a dusky pink and the sea to the north was a silver sparkle.

Ta-Kai flew that night. Along the coast. Mile upon mile, and westward. The desert eventually yielded to a vast river delta and swamp. Past that the terrain changed entirely and the dark green fuzz of jungle looming ahead. She dipped low into that dense canopy. Perched for hours in the heavy downpour, another night stalker among so many. In cat's guise she hunted and killed until sated. By dawn she turned about, glided back to the traders' camp by the city, entered her tent and waited for the mid-morning rush to pass.

The Lynx approached the city after noon. The place was in turmoil. Guards everywhere and people being flogged in the street. On the walls a line of freshly severed heads. The air stank of blood and fear. Those smells excited her. Curious, she entered the gates amid the chaotic bustle.

On closer inspection, Ta-Kai saw the gate guards were searching everyone. They appeared agitated and there were people crying out in pain, steel cutting flesh. Most likely a result of her actions the other night. *Best not draw unnecessary attention.*

Ta-Kai slipped away from the walls, watched for a time, pondered. She found a hidden spot and shifted her form, shaded from casual eyes by a buttress. Lifting high as a sparrowhawk and swooping breezy over the walls, her needle-sharp glance was on the row of heads spiked below.

She glided down through sunlight and breeze, flew past the temple, the sultan's palace. Settled in the gardens by the seat he used. *Selimo.* Always he frequented the gardens at this hour. No sign. She shifted back to human form and took her ease on the seat. He'd be here soon—his regular habit. *Their arrangement.* The three conspirators: the sorcerer in the north, his spy in the city, and the *Aikashi* assassin they employed.

No sign yet. She waited, her mood shifting to impatient anger. She faded back into the undergrowth twice as Crimson Guard crashed through on random patrols like so many peacocks disturbed by wild cats. Afternoon wore on; the sun blazed down above her head. She waited. *Maybe the sultan has detained him too?* More guards crashing through. Ta-Kai was getting restless, fidgety. Where was the fat fool?

Then she looked down and noticed the dried blood stains on the flagstones. She crouched low, sniffed. They were recent—an hour or so. *Just before I arrived here...*

Alerted, she crept through the gardens, her nose following the faint odor. The smell hit her at a midden outside the garden walls. She scrambled up a vine, lifted her leather-clad legs over and dropped down. The flies buzzing around her head. She didn't notice, saw the boots first. Then the fat soiled body of her contact, his throat slashed and gaping.

Interesting.

The sight pleased her greatly. She'd become bored, with her task completed. But now a new game had started. She would find who did this and why. Clearly those Crimson-clad fools were not up to the task. She sensed there were other professionals here. Like her.

Well…not like her. But efficient and daring. A worthy foe at last!

She pawed around the stinking body, finding nothing of interest. She would alert Caswallon. But in good time.

First let's have some fun…

Ta-Kai changed back into sparrowhawk form. She glided between palms, lifted over the walls and flew high above the city, her keen eyes watching all movement below. She circled, drifting back and forth on the thermals until she saw what she sought. Three figures climbing into a crack below the shadow of the wall.

Ta-Kai swooped down; a stone cast from above, plummeting, descending, and settling light as liquid on the street. She glimpsed a young woman and a boy before they vanished into the crack. But the third figure turned and saw her watching. She cried out in her bird voice, and swooped for his face. He ducked low and she left him there, reaching up again high above the city, feeling the joy of a new hunt.

Chapter 16 | Regroup

Corin cursed as the bird flashed past his face. *Bloody thing.* His nerves were shot bad enough without getting dive-bombed by shitehawks. They'd crept through the city, by way of the sewers. Not pleasant, but young Dully had responded quickly to his sisters' urgent message. He'd been excited, happy to see her.

The resourceful pair had known every crook and hideout before they reached the sewer. Even so, that had proved tricky with Crimson Guard everywhere. Corin had heard fighting and wondered how his friends were coping.

Crawling through the sewers didn't make for a fun afternoon but was better than getting poked at by heated steel. You had to stay positive in these situations. *Hold your nerve and keep your head.* Besides, his young companions weren't complaining.

Dully led them through culverts and holes, down to the city's belly. They'd emerged hard by the walls, waited in the dusty quiet of a deserted corner. Dully had scrambled out and run off. Returning quickly and nodding they come out. He'd led them to the crack in the walls, scarce wide enough for Corin.

"Hurry!" hissed the boy, his face just showing in the gloom ahead. A tunnel accessed via a culvert hidden by drains. Corin suspected smugglers had widened it.

But not enough for comfort. He climbed down, still cursing the bird for his ragged nerves, and crept on his knees behind the boy and his sister. They reached the far end, sunlight stabbed him but he glimpsed another crack. More of a drain hole, but with iron bars blocking escape.

Not good.

"Don't worry," Dully grinned at him. "I've been working on these bars for months—they're my way out of the city." Corin's eyes widened as Dully moved his nimble fingers along one of the bars, twisted it and the rod clattered on the ground.

"How?" Corin asked.

"Stole a hacksaw," Dully said. "Came down here whenever I could. Hard work but I've sawed through three. Always put them back so as not to cause suspicion."

"Quite the little smuggler, you are," Corin laughed.

"Among other things," the boy's sister said. There was a gap wide enough for Corin to squeeze through. Outside the sun hit him like a sizzling mallet. Late afternoon. Quiet. He guessed they were a long way from either gate. He heard a distant rumble that could only be the sea. Corin looked at Dully.

"Northside," the boy said. "I usually make for the dunes, follow them for a mile and then turn back towards the city cross-country. Slip inside one of the caravan camps."

"Why bother—I thought you were a pickpocket?"

"He finds the pockets hold more out here," the girl said.

"That and no Crimson," Dully added.

"So why stay in the city at all?" Corin asked as trotted alongside Dully and the girl, the shadow of walls shrinking behind them. Keep talking—that kept the fear of a crossbow bolt in your back at bay.

"Her," Dully nodded at his sister running on ahead.

"You tried to help her—a slave? What could you do?"

"Not much," Dully shrugged. "Her name's Talesa, though she'll never mention it. I call her Tally."

"Shame—pretty name."

"She's been through a lot," Dully said. "Worse than me. *Far worse*. Tally doesn't speak of those things they…"

"But you managed to get in," Corin glanced over his shoulder at the walls. *Out of bowshot now*. "That garden. Visit her regularly?"

"Most days."

Corin shook his head amazed at the courage of these young people. They reached the dunes, rested up for several minutes then walked for almost a mile before crossing through the dune shrub and entering the brown pastures surrounding the city.

"You'd best come with me," Corin said. "I'll introduce you to the rest of the team, though they're mostly a bunch of losers."

"Can't be as bad as the Crimson," Dully grinned at him. An hour later Corin arrived at his tent and smiled lovingly seeing Clouter perched against the table. Coly emerged, grinned at him and the boy, then shot an appraising glance at Talesa.

"Thought we might see you again, Master Dully," Coly said. "Who's the girl?" he asked Corin.

"My sister," Dully said defensively.

Coly flashed the boy a grin. "Good looking pair, you are. Stay away from Borgil."

"Who is Borgil?" Talesa asked when they were outside.

"That fat bastard with the horned helmet," Corin said, pointing to the axman, currently watching two of the others playing dice. The three turned as Corin approached.

"Still alive then," Borgil said.

"Aye—you disappointed?"

"Nope," Borgil said. "Didn't want to feel cheated." He glanced over the boy and rested his bloodshot eyes on Talesa. Those eyes lingered in that direction. "Who?"

"My new friends," Corin said. "Go near either of them and I'll fillet your ball sack. Understood?" Borgil just stared at him, and Corin laughed and left him to it.

"No sign of Hagan?" he asked Coly.

"Not yet."

"We'll give it until nightfall and then get moving," Corin said.

"Moving—where?" Dol placed his dice on the table and glanced up.

"South," Corin said. "There's a camp we need to raid."

"Oh, right," Dol returned to his cards but Rejen loomed over.

"Gold any nearer?" Rejen said.

"Depends," Corin told him.

"Fucking better be," Borgil said from somewhere close. Corin returned to his tent, the boy and his sister trailing him like faithful hounds.

"You two can sleep here," Corin told them before he closed his eyes and rolled on his blanket. It had been a long day so far.

"That man with the helmet's got it in for you," Talesa said. She sounded worried. Corin opened an eye, saw Dully poring over Clouter.

"Don't touch that," Corin said. Dully looked at him. "For your own sake," Corin smiled. "Clouter tends to bite."

"Clouter?" Talesa crinkled a brow.

"Every sword should have a name," Corin told her.

"It's massive," Dully was still gazing at the weapon. "You must be hugely strong."

"Tis more of a knack—now shut the fuck up and let me sleep."

"How can you sleep with that bad man out there?" Talesa said.

"Occupational hazard," Corin winked at her. "Besides, I have you two as guards." He closed his eyes again and this time nodded off. A boot woke him some time later. "Man approaching," Dully's voice in his ear. Corin's eyes winked open. Dark outside the tent.

"Hagan's back," Coly's face appeared at the canvas screen.

"Bout bloody time," Corin said, slipping into his boots and bidding the youngsters stay put. "We've a journey to plan," Corin told them. "You two can rest up here in the tents until we return. If we don't return then sell the tents and cookware and piss off to Cappel Cormac. It's a shithole but you'll be safer there than this place."

"We're coming with you," Dully said.

"No—you're not."

"What kept you?" Corin asked as he joined the others surrounding Hagan outside their circle of tents. Hagan's gray eyes flashed annoyance and then he shrugged.

"I waited until the fuss died down enough for me to slip outside the city."

"Through those gates?" Borgil said.

"No, you twat—I flew over the walls," Hagan said. "I persuaded the guards to let me out." He hefted a spear he'd brought along. "Skewered six of the bastards."

"And next they'll be searching these camps," Corin glared at him.

"What was I supposed to do—ask them for a favor?"

"Drop your trousers for all I care," Corin said. "You've brought the fucking hornet's nest down on us."

"Yeah, well—thought we were moving soon anyway," Hagan shrugged. "When are we going?"

"Five minutes ago," Corin said, and walked back inside his tent to tell his new friends they were joining him after all.

They left quietly, untied their beasts and guided them through the camps. The odd trader glanced their way but no one showed any interest. Just another party leaving early. Several had gone already due to the latest disturbance inside the city. Trade hadn't been good today.

Once outside the camp and hidden by a shadow of palms, the men mounted their camels. Dully shared one with his sister, Coly having got them a spare with some last-minute bartering.

Corin and Hagan were last to mount up. They watched the distant gates for a while until satisfied nothing was happening. Those dead guards could lie there for a while before the next watch found them. So Corin hoped.

"Ready?" He said to Hagan. The other man nodded and hoisted himself onto the camel's back.

"Yah!" Hagan shouted and the shadow of man and camel faded into night. Corin lingered a moment longer, a strange feeling of being watched upon him. He caught the briefest flicker of movement. And then he saw it. A large white cat. *An albino?* Dark clever eyes surveyed him coolly from beyond the palms.

I know those eyes...

The cat paced towards him calmly. Corin stood rooted. Then he reached for Clouter. The cat shape had shimmered and changed, from shadow to substance. A woman stood there. The woman from Rado's tavern. The girl Tashi, a smile on her lips.

Corin eased Clouter from its scabbard but stopped when the pale woman placed a finger to her lips. She was clad in midnight leather, two swords across her shoulders, long sleek pony-tail neatly rested on one shoulder. Knee length boots tucked over; Tashi wore wrist straps on arms, the glint of steel hinting blades. Her arms were folded as though waiting for him to make the move.

"It's you." Corin said.

"Yes," she nodded.

"Worked for Rado." Best he could do for the moment.

"Briefly, yes," she smiled, and he saw those neatly filed teeth. Strange how he hadn't seen those in the tavern. Thing a man notices most times.

"Where's your hostage?" Corin said.

"For you to find, handsome," she smiled at him again, a raw sensual smile. It lingered and he felt sudden trail of sweat beading down his back.

"Why are you doing this—must be more to it than gold?" She didn't answer, but seemed intrigued by the question. "Who are you?" Corin tried another tack. He couldn't hear the others. Needed to catch up.

"Because I like games," the woman who had once been Tashi winked at him and then faded back into night.

"You like hurting people, you mean? This is no game, Lady. I can promise you that much. Next time we meet it won't go well for you!"

"I cannot wait..." The voice trailed off like night breeze over sands. Corin let go of the camel's harness and thrashed about under the trees. No one there. No sign of any disturbance. But looking up he glanced a dark speck flicking across the moon. A second shape settled beside him.

Vervandi looked angry. "You are a fool to bait her," the redhead said. "That one is more than a match for your sword."

"We shall see," Corin said, feeling the customary dream state he always felt when Vervandi was close. "Besides, I have you looking out for me, don't I?"

"Don't count on it," Vervandi's green/gold gaze flashed at him from

the darkness. She became an owl, faded, wings drumming up into the night. Corin watched her go, wishing he could find a hole somewhere close filled with ale, sit inside and drink himself stupid.

Chapter 17 | The Clash in the Desert

Wake up—we're leaving," Ranysi's husky voice whispered in her ear. Nalissa opened her eyes. She'd been dreaming, for several hours rescued by a blissful sleep. An escape. She'd been walking through her father's gardens at Vioyamis, an autumn breeze lifting her hair, and birds chirping on the plum trees, those exploding with fruit. Her feet were bare and soft voices called out to her.

Those voices faded into Ranysi's hoarse whisper, and the horror, fear and dread came racing back shattering any memory of her dream. "What is it?" She managed after a moment's blinking.

"You need to get up, wash—and do it quickly," Ranysi placed a copper bowl of water on the table beside her. Nalissa stared at it.

"It's nighttime...what?"

"Almost dawn," Ranysi looked up as the tent flap was pulled back and Ralco Ren's monstrous face appeared. Nalissa bit her lip, held back the scream she felt rising inside. "We're ready, give us a minute please," Ranysi said. The giant mute glared at her, at Nalissa, and then dropped the flap again.

"Eat this," Ranysi placed a ball of dough in her hand, cold and congealed. "We're moving out again."

"What...?"

"Just fucking eat it," Ranysi looked anxious, scared even. A look that didn't suit her. "Pray we survive this day," she muttered.

Nalissa stuffed the cold bun in her mouth, tasteless and doughy but it settled her stomach, and the cold water splashing on her face chased the last hint of sleep away. She dressed, quickly.

Outside, the camp was shrouded in dark. Shadows lifted and fell away as a shrinking white moon rolled through a thin veil of cloud. Somewhere close by a bird called three times, a lonely sound in that desolate place. Lonely as her heart.

She walked behind Ranysi to where the camels were stationed. Nalissa heard men snoring inside the other tents. Then she saw him, Dracal. The master. He looked at her askance, and hinted them hurry, the giant Ralco looming up behind him, leading a train of four camels, the reins looped in his massive fists.

"What's happened?" Nalissa said, then regretted it as Ralco's bucket sized fist unraveled from the reins with lightning speed and struck her face, a slap that knocked her teeth together.

She spat at him and he cuffed her again. This time she fell to her knees.

"Enough!" Dracal hissed at his overseer. "Time to get moving." Ralco nodded, turned his back on the girls and led the camels through the tents, passed the dying campfire into a knot of brush.

Ranysi helped Nalissa to her feet, and the two followed the men until they reached a quiet place to mount up. They left the camp, rode for an hour across difficult terrain until the sun rose like a giant ruby in the east, lighting the way ahead. Nobody spoke. Nalissa's head was hurting from the blows, and her half-healed lip had split open again.

She had two choices. *Escape or slit my wrists. Father, have you forgotten your child?*

***

Rylen Snake Eyes rolled to his feet and kicked off the blanket, his sharp instincts telling him something was amiss. He shoved his head through the tent flap. No one about. The fire had gone out and he saw no sentry on stag.

Alarm bells sounding in his head, Rylen strapped the broadsword to his belt and trousers, and ventured out into the cold desert morning. The first thing he saw was the vulture pecking out Gossil's eyes. The man charged with the last two hours' watch. Murdered. His throat gaping and eyes glazed over, a look of stunned surprise showing.

Those dead eyes stared accusingly at Rylen as he chased the birds off. Next up he checked the camels. Gone—predictably. Dracal had said they'd talk about things last night. That hadn't happened. Instead Rylen and the boys had smoked into the late hours, forgetting the slaver and their current situation as the hemp laid heavy on them.

A stupid mistake, and he blamed himself. Dracal had left an unusually generous amount of weed in the mess tent. They'd taken the hint without wondering why. *My fault, Stron wouldn't have fallen for that ruse.*

Rylen woke the others: down to eighteen men now. But they were mercenaries, hardened killers, not cowards like Dracal the slaver, running after his own tail. Besides, where the fuck could they run to?

"What now?" Duart said. The stocky Morwellan was seated on a rock sharpening his double-headed ax, some of the others gathered around. Long Thom, the ranger, Grizzle-Jaw Grillen, Poley Peet— named after the legendary length of his organ, the rest walking over.

"We wait and see who's coming," Rylen said. "And someone needs to bury Gossil before those fucking birds give our position away." They were circling up there, a dozen perhaps more.

Duart held his position on the rock. "Slaver lose his nerve?"

"Looks like it," Rylen said. "Must have shat himself in the wee hours. Left with that bastard mute, only took a couple of girls."

"That mean we're slavers now?" Long Thom grinned, seeming to like the idea.

"Until we sell 'em—yes," Rylen said. "There's what... thirty or more, and most are lasses. We'll take em to Cappel. Flog them at the markets and then stay drunk for a month."

"First we have to get to Cappel with our heads still on our shoulders," Duart said, switching his attention to the second blade. "That bastard Dracal wouldn't throw his livelihood away without good reason."

"He fucked up in the city is all," Rylen said. "You worry too much, Duart. The Crimson never leave Sedinadola. And even if they do the tossers can't fight. They're highly overrated. You know they hardly drew blood in the war, except to massacre villages and execute prisoners, then turn on our lads when the dirty work was done."

"We're eighteen," Duart grumbled. "Could be a hundred fucking lancers coming our way."

"Best we get ready then," Rylen Snake Eyes grinned at the axman. "Don't want to disappoint them."

They buried Gossil a good distance from the camp. The slaves were fed and watered and ordered to lie low inside the tents.

It was a grim predicament, but Rylen had endured worse. They had water and food, enough for his men and the slaves. If some of the male ones died, so what? The girls, they'd look after.

Now to wait...

Some of the lads diced, others practiced steel on steel. Duart worked on his ax while Rylen shut his eyes and drifted off as the mid-morning heat fell heavy on the valley.

***

Ralance Jago called a halt as they rode closer to a ridge of brown hills, the odd rocky outcrop spilling down to the dry river bed they were negotiating. Rough country down here, and good for ambush too. Best they approach with caution.

"How far?" Jago asked his second, Coralion.

"Couple of miles as my memory serves—Can you not smell the water?"

"I smell death," Jago looked up into the deep blue above and saw tiny shapes circling. Buzzards or vultures. Coralion saw where he was looking and grinned.

"Perhaps we are too late," the captain said.

"More likely some dead animal," Jago said. "Spread the word back. We proceed with caution from now on. Take our time. I want every man watching that ridge for movement or glint of steel."

"Dracal's a slaver, not a veteran campaigner."

"He has those with him—doubtless they've advised him be watchful." They rode slowly, the horses picking their way around stones and pebbles, the scree from the ridge above. Morning faded into early afternoon, the brown shimmer of heat like wax melting their faces, the red cloaks heavy and bodies sore.

The Crimson seldom left the city. But General Ralance Jago needed to make an impact. His men needed honing; they needed a kill. Gortansez had been too docile, content to preen his feathers and sit comfortable with the Crimson's reputation. Jago was different. He had plans for his soldiers. The Sultan would see a marked improvement. Today was the start of a glorious campaign.

***

"And here they are," Long Thom said, the eyeglass thrust against his lids.

"How many?" Rylen asked, as they lay flat on the southern end of the long ridge concealing camp and oasis, the palms shading the valley below.

"Fifty, maybe sixty?" Thom took another look.

"Hide that fucking thing before it gives our position away," Duart nudged Thom in the ribs. "Sun catches that glass, be like a big flag saying 'Here we are tosspots!'"

"I've already said you worry too much, Dui," Rylen told the axman. "Relax. Those boys are green as lily stalks, and way over-confident to boot. City dwellers. They might outnumber us three to one, but we hold the position and have surprise on our side." He was about to add something else when the dust kicked up a foot to his right, the crossbow bolt just missing them.

"Told you," Duart almost smiled.

They rolled back, slid down the far side of the ridge and then hurried into camp. "Here they come!" Rylen yelled as he sprinted for the tents and noticed with satisfaction that the lads had got the makeshift barricade ready.

They waited several minutes then the thunder of hooves on stone announced company had arrived. The Crimson carried spears, lances and shields, though some had crossbows, and bolts were whizzing their way, striking the turned wagons, all missing.

They stopped at the edge of camp. A line of red-cloaked pretty boys, their armor dazzling and hard to set eyes on. A single rider rode out. He wore gauntlets, a scimitar swinging at his side.

Long Thom nocked arrow to string, pulled back. He grinned at Rylen who nodded. "Kill that silly bastard."

***

Coralion saw his general cry out and pitch from his horse the arrow sticking in his chest. So much for Ralance Jago's rising career. *Guess I'm the general now.* Coralion slammed his scimitar free of its sheath and spurred his horse to canter past the dying general.

"Take them!" Coralion screamed, looking back at his men as he thundered toward the makeshift barricade of wagons and broken-up lumber. In seconds they were with him, a red blaze of fire streaking towards the treacherous enemy, hidden behind their screens. "I want prisoners!" Coralion yelled, then the arrow took him in the knee and he fell from his horse.

***

Corin looked at the ground as he led the camel to water. Cart tracks and camel shit. Charred faggots from abandoned fires. A large organized camp, recently deserted. Dracal must be in trouble. That meant Nalissa would be in even greater danger. They needed to make haste. Time was running out for the merchant's daughter.

"looks like the whole cavalcade went south," Dol said. He'd been scouting at the southern end of the camp. Followed the dry river's course."

"How long?" Hagan was looking up at the sky.

"Two days," Dol said. "And they have a troop of Crimson on their tale. Hoof prints clearly visible covering over some of the other marks."

"The Crimson—out here?" Corin shook his head.

"Only riders allowed expensive horses as I recall," Dol said. "Shod shoeprints in the dirt. Your slaver must have upset the big man in the city." Corin thought of Selimo, but this had happened earlier. There was another factor playing out here, and even more the need for haste.

He vaulted onto the camel's back. "Best get going," Corin said. They looked at him surprised. "You want that gold—or what?" They joined him and rode south.

It was almost dusk when they saw the birds far off, over a hundred circling. Corin had a sinking feeling in his belly. *Nalissa...* She wasn't dead—he had to hold on to that fading hope.

They filed along the dry river bed, eight hard-faced men, and two young people caught in their midst. Corin hadn't had time to think about Dully and the girl, his mind had been preoccupied with the Lynx's visit last night, and Vervandi's words, and then his fear of what awaited them ahead.

He signaled the others forward and waited for the last two camels where Dully sat alongside his sister, her towing the pack animal behind.

"We part ways here," Corin smiled at the pair.

"We're with you," Dully said, his face anxious.

"Nope," Corin smiled. "Your responsibility is with your sister, Dully. You need to protect her from wild animals, and bad people. You cannot stay with us. We're riding into battle."

"We're coming," Dully said.

"I can look after myself," his sister added.

"Look," Corin said, aware the other men were leaving them behind. "I need both hands for my sword. I won't be able to watch out for you. There's a girl I need to save, might be too late already but I have to try, and I stand more chance of succeeding without worrying about you too."

"A girl?" Talesa said.

"A slave...now."

"Then you had better get going—hadn't you," Talesa had a tear in her eye.

"Make for Cappel Cormac," Corin said. "Mention my name— or Hagan's— at *The Green Duck*. You'll be safe there until I return. *Safer than staying here*," he added under his breath. "Take the pack animal and cut across country. Stay away from the cities until you reach *The Silver Strand* beyond Syrannos. You should have no problems entering Cappel Cormac during daylight. It's a crowded filthy city, unlike Sedinadola.

"*The Green Duck*," Dully nodded, but still looked unhappy.

"Look after your sister," Corin told him. "I lost mine."

"That was careless," Dully said. Talesa had already turned back her camel, her face hidden in her hood.

Corin felt a pang of sorrow. He smiled sadly. "Aye, Dully. That it was," he said." Corin watched brother and sister ride back along the track, the pack beast clomping behind them.

Images of Ceilyn flashed through his mind. A beloved sister lost so long ago. Vanished in the desert beyond. Alive or just bones bleached by sun—he'd never know. *I'm not failing this time.* Corin turned his own animal around. "Yah!"

***

Rylen tore the lance from his side and crawled up the slope, the flies clustering around him. He'd found a gourd, drank deep, but the wound was deeper. The Crimson had proved unpredictably savage, their wounded officer having roused them into a fury after the death of their leader.

The fight had lasted an hour, no more. The makeshift camp was strewn with corpses, large birds down there feeding on flesh. Rylen had had to get away. He'd gouged out the last spearman's eyes with broken finger-nails.

The fighting had been hard, a close call. Their initial charge had done for three of the lads; he'd seen Poley Peet fall with a bolt through his eye. Grillan had been torn open by three spears, he saw that happening again as a flash of images returned to him.

Another memory—Duart sitting on a rock, maybe the same rock he'd sat on this morning. Only difference was his head was missing. The others? Most likely dead, and the slaves left to starve in the wild.

They'd held their own, done well. The Crimson were dead, He'd killed the last one after taking the lancer's weapon in his flank. The pain screamed at him.

Not dying here. No bird pecking my flesh

Rylen crawled for over an hour until he slid down a slope and crashed into shrubby thorns. These trapped him and he lacked the strength to fight any longer. He closed his eyes, passed out.

Cool water slapped his face. His lips were parched and cracking, head throbbing as though beaten by hammers, and only one eye opened. He saw a shadow leaning over him.

"Still alive," a rough voice said. A long face hovered over him, scarred, wild hair beneath a hood.

"Who are you?" Rylen wriggled his eyelid until the other one opened.

"Corin an Fol."

"I've heard that name…" Rylen tried to move his head but the pain tore into his side. He passed out again briefly. When he came to another man stood over him. Lean, hard gray eyes, unsmiling. Another northerner.

"My mates?"

"Torn up by birds, me old son," Gray Eyes said. "I expect you'll join them soon—those wound looks bad."

"Not planning on dying," Rylen spat red phlegm on sandy soil. "Need a drink." The other man who'd called himself Corin an Fol reached down with his water gourd.

"I said I need a *drink*," Rylen said, closing his eyes again. The pain was getting worse.

A third man appeared, lanky, lopsided grin, bare headed, long sandy hair loosely tied back and lifting in the stiffening breeze. The sun had set and night would fall upon them shortly.

The fair-haired one reached down with a flask. "Just a drop mind," he said.

"Don't share it with that bastard, Coly—what's the matter with you?" Gray Eyes snatched the flask away but Pony-Tail offered it to his lips again.

"He's one of our own, Hagan," Coly said. "A northerner."

"Serving a slaver," Corin an Fol said.

"Good point," Coly took the grog away before Rylen got a taste. "Where is he?"

"Who?" Rylen said between chokes. "Give me that drink, for fuck's sake…Please. I'm not feeling my best."

"Tell us where your master is and you can finish that," Scarface Corin said. "We found slaves, pitiful things, cringing inside that canvas. Lots of dead bodies too, but no fucking slaver. And more importantly no sign of the person I need to find. Where are they!" Corin grabbed Rylen's tunic and pulled him up, the pain ripping at his side again.

"Gone," Rylen said, coughing up blood. They waited for him to finish.

"Gone where?" Corin said when Rylen finally ceased his coughing.

"Don't know—bastard stabbed the sentry last night and took two of the girls along with his henchman."

"That's all?" The men's faces grew blurry. Someone thrust the flask in his lips and Rylen sucked at the fiery liquid.

"Thanks," he said, "I'll sleep for a while now before I get my breath back." He closed his eyes and felt tingles along his spine like tiny fingers. They pulled him down hard into heavy nothingness.

Chapter 18 | A New Lead

Corin stared down at the dead mercenary lying at his feet. Tough bastard. The man's guts were half hanging out and he'd crawled for quarter of a mile. Bad way to go—even for a lowlife killer.

"Snake Eye dead?" The voice came from Borgil walking up the slope, his ax slung across a shoulder.

"You knew this bastard?" Hagan asked Borgil, Corin not being on speaking terms with the axman.

"Used to," Borgil grunted, kicking the corpse and making the flies dance. "Rylen the crafty. Good with a knife. Snake Eyes they called him, on account of his cold heart."

"Didn't know Kettle Head had a brother," Corin said to Hagan, who barked a laugh. "The others?"

"Fifteen dead, and three score Crimson feeding the carrion."

"They won't like that when word gets back," Coly said. "What now, Corin an Fol, and what about those slaves down there?"

Corin sighed. *No Nalissa.* He'd been hoping this would end today. At least she was still alive, or likely to be. But why would Dracal take her and leave the others. Nalissa was a beauty, but so were some of the other girls he'd seen.

"I don't have time to spend worrying about them," Corin said eventually.

"We could sell them at market," Hagan said, and Borgil nodded enthusiastically,

"You're as callous as he was," Corin eyeing Rylen's corpse. He left the others standing there and walked back down to where the rest of Hagan's men were gathered around the main tent cluster, Dracal's slaves still hiding within.

"What's happening?" Rejen asked Corin, but he ignored the redhead and pulled back the flap to the largest tent. He counted six girls in there.

"Out you come," Corin told them.

Rejen laughed when the women staggered out into the sun, their terrified, grimy faces looked like deer on edge of flight.

"Recreation time!" Rejen said, and some of the men laughed. "Pick your girl lads," Rejen reached for one but Corin stopped him.

"Shut the fuck up," Corin said. "We're not slavers."

"They're captives of war—contraband," Rejen's smile had fled his lips and the color drained from that ruddy face.

"You're not touching any of them," Corin's hand was on Clouter's hilt. Rejen reached for his sword.

"Leave it, Rej," Hagan said as he joined them. "Corin's promised us gold. These wenches will only slow us down."

Rejen said nothing but his eyes were on Corin. *Another enemy to watch.* But he didn't have the time.

Corin studied the women. The rest had emerged from the other tents and half a dozen men were among them. Two of these looked like former warriors, black skinned, scarred and tough as wire.

"Your name?" Corin asked the larger of the two.

"Srolgo."

"Handle a sword?" The man's face lit up and a savage joy glinted his eyes.

"I was a gladiator in the Games at Vendel City, killed four men before the Yamondons slew our masters. Before that I was a soldier on the front. Survived six campaigns."

"I only asked if you could use a fucking sword," Corin said. "Don't want to hear about your entire career. Your friend here looks useful. Can matey fight?" The smaller man nodded fiercely. "Excellent," Corin said. "You two good fellows are charged with leading your companions to safety. That means staying the fuck clear of Sedinadola City. Understand?"

Strolgo nodded but the other slaves gathered outside the tents looked confused, and worried, as though exchanging one nightmare for another. "You're free to leave anytime," Corin said. "I suggest you use this night as a gift," he said. "Get away, find a ship, steal a horse—whatever works."

He left them then — he had his own matters to which he needed to attend. Hagan and Coly followed him, and after a moment Strolgo too with the smaller man tagging alongside.

"You need to watch your back with that Rejen," Coly warned him. Corin wasn't listening. The three of them were scanning the brush and rocks for signs of Dracal's exit.

"He'll have made for the coast." They turned, saw Strolgo standing with brawny arms folded, the smaller wiry one beside him.

"You still here?" Corin said.

"Wanted to thank you," Strolgo said. "Didn't much like being a slave—it's been a bad seven years."

"Sorry to hear that," Coly said. "But we're a tad occupied, old chap."

"Morazzo here can help you," Strolgo said, and the smaller man nodded. "He's southern Vendeli — a sailor from the distant ice lands. Says he knows where Dracal went."

Corin stopped, looked at the smaller man. "That so?"

Morazzo smiled revealing the two teeth left in his mouth. "I'll sailed these waters as a smuggler—it's how I was caught...eventually," he sounded bitter, disappointed with himself. "There's a cove not that far away, along the coast twenty miles west of the Sultan's city."

"A cove?" Hagan asked.

"Hidden. A secret known only to local smugglers and Crenise Pirates."

"Crenise Pirates?" Corin said, the scowl curling his lip as memory stole upon him.

"Dracal purchases slaves from them to avoid taxes in the city," Morazzo said. "They have a hideout offshore, a small island. Conduct regular business with our former master." Strolgo spat beside his friend.

"How far?" Corin said.

"Can get you there by morning if we leave right away," Morazzo said. "We need only find the coast road and I'll know where we are. The Trading Station should be quiet at first light."

"Trading Station?" Corin shook his head, not liking the sound of that.

"The cove lies three miles beyond it, well hidden," Morazzo said. "The Station serves to check merchants travelling from Golt have the correct passes. But the guards there are in on the secret. Dracal and the Crenise pay them for their silence and discretion. We can persuade those guards to tell us when Dracal got there, and whether his allies the Crenise are around."

"Sounds like a plan," Corin flashed Morazzo a grin.

"I'm coming too," Strolgo said, as Corin and Hagan told the others their plan. It met with some enthusiasm as the Crenise pirates were rumored to be rich, and if they had a stash hereabouts it would doubtless be worthwhile. But Corin had other reasons to punish the Crenise. Old memories flared back at him. The raid, his father's dying face. *His mother...*

"You're charged with saving those womenfolk," Corin told Strolgo, but the big former warrior shook his head.

"The men there are dependable," he said. "Two are former hunters, and some of the girls are too. Jarmei's good with a spear and knife. We're a tough group. The desert won't kill my friends."

"I hope not," Corin said. "But why risk your neck for us? You're free, and your friend here can assist us greatly with his guidance, but you we do not need."

"There's a man I need to kill," Strolgo said.

"I'll deal with Dracal," Corin said. "I'll need him alive to find out who his friends are."

"I'm not talking about the slaver. It's Ralco Ren I'm going to kill."

"And who's he?" Coly asked, but Strolgo didn't answer.

"Must be the overseer who went with him," Hagan said to Corin.

"Doesn't matter," Corin said. "Past time we got started."

***

Nalissa's eyes jolted open as the animal carrying her stopped. She heard voices, saw the distant shapes of men approaching, their faces buried in hoods and djellabas. They looked angry, questioning.

Huge Ralco stayed put with Ranysi and Nalissa herself as Dracal walked over calmly to confer with these men.

"I remember this place," Ranysi whispered in Nalissa's ear when Ralco turned away. "A tariff of sorts—he's done business here before. We're near the ocean I think.'

The ocean. Nalissa felt a stab of yearning. One sight of the ocean and she knew she would cry. That way lay home, freedom, *everything*. Dracal stood talking to the men for several minutes while they waited. Eventually he turned back and the others walked back to some distant huts and a low-roofed building resembling a shoddy tavern.

Dracal muttered something inaudible to Ralco and the giant

nodded. He jolted the camels' harness and the beasts moved forward. They were on a road, Nalissa noted as the morning light promised another blistering day. They'd rested up for most of yesterday and traveled under darkness, Dracal seemed to know this country well.

They'd only followed the road for twenty minutes when Dracal motioned to his man, ushering them divert into a cluster of brush fanned by tall palms nodding in the wind. And that was when she smelt it. The ocean. A stiff sea breeze, and moments later Nalissa caught glance of clear blue water, a sleepy cove far below.

Dracal motioned they dismount. Ralco Ren shouldered the belongings and supplies, as Dracal lashed the camels to a post obviously provided for the purpose. The efficiency and speed of his actions hinted the slaver did this regularly.

He is meeting someone—but who?

It was all she could do not to cry out in despair at the sight of those breakers brushing sand far below. A long climb down, steps cut into stone—several missing—and then a knotted roped descending and vanishing into thick dense carpets of green. They reached the bottom. The sea scarce a hundred yards away, the sting of brine salting her face and mixing with the tears.

"Now we wait," Dracal said to Ralco. "Let the girls sleep. I want them looking their best, especially that one," he jerked his head at Nalissa. "The Crenise will have heard of her father. I'll get twice the money the Sultan's people would cough up." He wandered off and lit his hookah. Nalissa wished she could follow him and cut out his liver.

She closed her eyes, let the hot sun and sound of the waves steady her nerves. This game wasn't over yet. She could wait. Opportunity would present itself—to kill these evil men or slit her own throat. Either way an escape from her current predicament.

***

Dracal let the waves lull his senses and drift through his mind like the smoke he inhaled. Behind, the girls were sleeping—or else pretending to. Ranysi was sharp, which was the reason he'd brought her—to keep an eye on the other one. Stop the girl from doing anything stupid. The Crenise would have got word by now, those tax robbers at the Trading Station having sent a bird. The pirates' crag was just offshore; he'd been over there once. A village of sorts: inns, houses—even a large wooden hall. The Crenise had a new leader these days, and the pirates had become better organized, almost a private army.

He'd give it an hour or two, then venture down to the hidden jetty, look for those familiar triangular sails. Once he'd got rid of the girls, he and Ralco would fade back into the desert for a time. Make slowly for the rebel town of Agmandeur where they could exist comfortably on their proceeds, staying clear of Barakani's artful eye.

He leaned back against a mound of sand and smiled. The smile fell from his face when Dracal spotted a tern falling like lead from the sky. It didn't look natural— too fast. The bird settled on a rack of weed close by the water, and started hopping about. It lifted again and landed on a large driftwood log, familiar dark eyes pinning him.

***

Craften of Storne steered his vessel toward the shoreline, his twenty men working the oars along either side. Shallow waters here; he'd lowered the sail, but left it flapping long enough for those waiting on that beach to see.

An easy hop from South Town, the Lord Assassin's new hideout down here. Prince Rael had had it furnished with the best material. There was no shortage of ale, food, and lively women for his men. They often spent months down here, far away from the High King's justice.

The shoreline swelled, a mass of green parting to reveal a yellow strip, the beach, and at its southern end a wooden jetty—a square spike thrusting out across the waves. A lone figure stood there, dressed in desert apparel, the wind flapping his loose garments back and forth.

Dracal the Slaver was well known to Craften and his crew, having been their guest on the island once. He'd even met the Rogue Prince himself, Craften's leader, Rael the Cruel.

But this sudden call out was unexpected. The word *hostage* was mentioned in the note clamped around the pigeon's foot.

They heaved to and lines were cast. Dracal's huge mute appeared and grabbed one and tied off to the jetty. Craften leaped ashore and embraced the slaver. That done, he looked past and saw the two women standing at the far end of the jetty.

"For me?" Craften grinned.

"Your master, Prince Rael," Dracal said. "The tall one is a gift; the other more of a hostage." He'd stopped talking suddenly as a third woman had appeared behind the girls and was strolling towards them with what looked like two swords hanging from her back.

"Who is that?" Craften said before the crossbow bolt thudded into his chest and he crashed off the jetty sinking into warm blue water.

Chapter 19 | Blood and Steel

Silon loaded a second bolt, aimed and fired, but the two other men on the jetty had dived for cover. The larger man was swimming at speed back to the shore, the other, crawling low and making for the refuge of the ship.

Silon ran, working the crossbow with deft fingers; he heard screams, saw a girl running—not Nalissa. A black-skinned girl, tall athletic, sprinting along the beach. Silon couldn't catch her, but he saw the huge man break free of the combers and leap after the girl.

Another scream, close by. That sounded like Nalissa. *Where is she?* More shouts announced the Crenise had realized this was a lone attacker and were pouring back onto the jetty. Some carried bows and two levelled them at Silon, now a target on the beach.

"Nalissa!" He dived, and rolled, an arrow thudding into the sand, a second following. *Nalissa.* For the briefest second, he glimpsed her, emerging from behind a shadow of palms, her beautiful face, torn, distraught, and amazed at seeing him there.

"Father!" He heard her voice then another arrow thudded to his right, and the shouts announced the Crenise were on the beach, yards away, and sprinting toward him.

"Run!" Silon yelled at his daughter before turning on his toes and sprinting in zig-zags for cover behind the brush and shelter of cliffs.

He reached a wall of stone. The shouts were nearer, closing fast. Silon tossed the crossbow aside; he needed both hands for this.

He climbed, pulled his body up, scraped knees and cut hands, but rolled onto a plinth a dozen feet above the first pirate now emerging from the beach. "Up there!" the man yelled as two others joined him and started to climb.

"Cut him off by the path!" Another voice called from down by the jetty. Silon climbed again, scurrying through brush, angling over and up the sandstone cliffs, slipping as the rock crumbled beneath his feet and fingers.

He reached another ledge. He was safe for the moment and out of sight, but a long way from his tethered horse and further still from Nalissa. He heard a woman scream again. Too far away to tell if it was her.

Silon sunk to his knees. He'd failed, blown his one chance to save her. Now she was lost to him forever. *No! I will find her again.* He waited a minute, then another. The shouts were no nearer, and sounded confused as though something new was happening.

Silon broke free of his cover, and climbed again. This time he didn't stop until he'd crested the ridge, and ran back to the lane that led to the Trading Station, his horse further back toward the beach. Too late to worry about that.

Armed only with a knife, his robe and headscarf torn and grimy, Silon wouldn't admit defeat. He'd get her back—somehow.

***

It had happened so fast Nalissa was still reeling from the shock of it. She'd been standing under the palms, having fled the jetty area, her mind still groggy from a half doze. She'd heard the shout, seen Dracal's contact struck by something, witnessed the pirate's body falling in the water.

Ranysi had reacted fast, running headlong for the far end of the beach, while Nalissa had stood there, frozen, mind numb. Then she'd seen him.

Father.

For one impossible, agonizing moment—his dark eyes pleading she join him. His voice calling out to her. But the men from the ship had rushed down to the beach and were firing arrows at him, causing Father flee from her sight.

Ignored and forgotten for a moment she'd followed the pursuers, briefly glimpsed her father again, climbing up through shale and cliff, a small anxious figure, those terrible men clambering after him. She'd lost sight of them all, and mind racing with emotions, staggered back along the beach, a vague thought of escape framing the edge of her mind, chased down by the fear that father was dead, or would be by nightfall.

My fault—I'm such a fool. Oh Father, so sorry.

She forced her legs to run. Too late. Ralco caught her on the beach and lifted her screaming and kicking into his massive grip, squeezing hard so her ribs felt like they were cracking. She blacked out.

***

Captain Coralion looked up at the sky where birds still circled. He knew he should be dead, the arrow stuck fast in his knee, the pain of it fading as nausea and giddiness pushed him to the brink of void.

He'd crawled out from under his dead horse's body. Looked around. Birds eating corpses, nothing else moving. Dark. *Got to report this atrocity—Jago's fault.*

Screaming at the pain, he'd found an abandoned spear and used it to pull himself to his feet, the arrow jutting through his knee, sitting amid the cartilage. Coralion used his elbows, heaving his battered body toward the distant shadow of a horse. The lone beast stood silent as the night around them.

Coralion, had mounted on the third attempt, and somehow managed to stay in saddle. He guided the beast out of the valley, the dead eyes of his men watching him in judgment, their faces trapped by moonlight.

In a dream state, sunk low over the saddle, Coralion rode back to the city, the constant sips from the water gourd barely keeping him conscious. That and the fury and disbelief of what had happened in the pass.

He reached the gates and the guards took him in. An hour later a detachment of two hundred riders left the city tasked with scouring the countryside from oasis to road. They patched up Coralion's leg and he rode out at dawn. A hero determined to make up for Ralance Jago's folly, and avenge the atrocity of the valley.

His leg strapped in a splint, Coralion took the coast road riding east, two score riders filing behind him. Let the others do the difficult work. He would meet up with them at the Trading Station on the Golt road, after he had questioned the guards posted there.

***

Dawn drew a line of pink ahead. Corin saw the thin ribbon of road, and glimmer of ocean beyond. Ten weary men; they rode out onto the cobbled surface and guided their beasts east, the sun rising behind them lighting their way.

They dismounted at a turn of the road half mile short from the trading station. Morazzo warning they were close. Coly and Dol stayed with the horses, whilst the other seven accompanied Corin, clambering and creeping through dune and brush, flanking the road, and arriving at the trading station unannounced.

"How many?" Corin crouched low and saw no sign of movement, except the three camels outside the furthest tent. A small affair, several tents circled the road, and a low round stone building bridged it, a trail of smoke rising from its midst.

"Four, maybe six," Morazzo said. "They'll be inside the main building—cooler in there, now the sun's showed his face."

"Time to pay a visit," Corin grinned. "Remember we need one fellow alive." They sprinted, keeping low and fast covering the short distance in seconds. Corin hissed at Hagan and Rejen to check those tents, while he and the others made for the round building.

They hustled close around the door, the camels tied in the corner by the last tent. "Ready?" Corin said. Even Borgil smiled. "On three, then… One, two. Three!" Borgil's ax split the door asunder and they rushed inside.

Shadows leapt away from a table. Corin glimpsed Borgil's ax falling and a man screaming as his arm was hewed off. A face emerged before him; he stabbed it. The man yelled, fell away. "Get that bastard!" Corin yelled seeing a shadow make for the door. Hagan appeared and struck the fleeing guard with his sword pommel knocking him sprawling.

"Tents are empty," Hagan said, stepping inside. "Someone, please stop him," he added as Corin turned and saw Borgil hewing the head from the last survivor.

"Five dead," Strain the Rope said, as he and Dilan persuaded Borgil to stop swinging his ax before one of them got whacked.

"What about him?" Corin hinted the guard sprawled on his face by Hagan's feet. "Doesn't look that good."

"I only cuffed him," Hagan said, and kicked the body until a voice groaned. "See—he's bright as roses in sunshine." Hagan reached down and hauled the remaining guard to his feet. "Hello mate, we've some questions for you. Answer promptly and you get to keep your head." The guard blinked at him.

Corin signaled Morazzo to come and question the guard. They'd only got a grunt out of him when Coly appeared, his face anxious and eyes wide in the gloom of the round house.

"Crimson," Coly said. "Riding this way."

"Fuck—you sure?" Corin said.

"Red cloaks, shiny mail and posh horses," Coly said. "Don't know who else that might be."

"How far?"

"Five minutes—max."

"That's not good," Hagan said. "Someone must have survived the fight yesterday. I thought you checked, Borgil—you, useless twat."

"I did."

"What do we do?"

"Get the fuck away," Rejen suggested.

"Too late," Corin said gazing out the broken door where a trail of dust announced the imminent arrival of the Crimson Guard.

Corin counted twenty-five riders, the armor gleaming in the early morning sun. "Best get ready," he said. "Going to be another busy morning."

"So glad I hooked up with you, Corin an Fol," Hagan said. "Life was a tad monotonous before."

"We are eight against twenty-five," Coly said as they all watched the column arrive in orderly fashion. They hadn't noticed anything amiss and rode slowly with confidence, the leader stiff in his saddle.

"Ten," Strolgo stood beside Morazzo. Both had extra swords in their hands taken from the dead men, and were smiling.

"Our kind of odds," Morazzo said. "I've enough rage bottled inside to murder them all."

"Excellent," Corin said. "Here's your chance, they've seen us. Good luck."

"What do you mean—*good luck*?" Hagan and Coly stared at him.

"You need to keep those bastards occupied while these two lads come with me to find the girl."

"You're having a laugh," Coly said. "You can't leave us here. Corin—we're in the shit already."

"You'll manage," Corin said. "I'm sorry, but I've got to find Nalissa before that bastard slaver sells her on." He turned, signaled the two ex-slaves follow. "Hold them off, I'll return soon as."

"Bastard," Hagan said.

"What did you expect?' This came from Borgil, beside him. Corin ignored them both. His obligations lay elsewhere.

"Horse?" Strolgo said as he sprinted alongside Corin.

"No time, besides they'll have discovered them. How far now?"

"A mile," Morazzo said. "You'll spot the cut in the bush, a path and steps leading down steep. Another mile and we're on the beach."

"Come on then," Corin said as they distanced themselves from the trading station, shouts and cusses replaced by the clash of steel as the Crimson caught up with Hagan's men. Corin didn't feel bad about leaving them. He lacked the time.

Nalissa was all that mattered. You had to be decisive in this life. Hesitate and you're a dead man. *Sorry, Hagan.*

***

Ralco dragged Nalissa for half a mile before Dracal appeared with Ranysi struggling, his knife pinned to her throat.

"Bring that slut here," the slaver said, and the brute carried Nalissa across to him and dropped her unceremoniously on the hard sand. Nalissa lay there, too stunned and exhausted to move.

The slaver shoved Ranysi across to Ralco, who seized her by the hair. "Kill her if she struggles," he told his henchman. Ralco nodded, his bug eyes eager.

Dracal turned his back on them and stared down at Nalissa, his expression merciless. "Caused me trouble you have, bitch." He kicked her in the stomach and Nalissa doubled up in pain.

"Who was that would-be assassin?" he kicked her a second time and Nalissa cried out. "Speak whore, or I'll rip that tongue out."

"My father," Nalissa spat the words out. "He'll be back, doesn't give up. Never." She braced herself for another kick but instead her tormentor was laughing.

"That was Silon the merchant?" Dracal stared back along the beach. "That fool? How very disappointing, and I thought your father an intelligent man. Those allies of mine will cut his heart out and cook it, after they've removed other parts. He killed their captain— the Crenise won't like that."

"Shame it wasn't you," Nalissa spat again.

"No harm done," Dracal said as though he hadn't heard her. "I'll sell you and Ranysi to those lads—they'll pay double for you now. Done me a favor, girl." He laughed again, then started as a shadow past over them. Nalissa thought she saw a shape settle in the shimmer of sand a little way off.

Hard to tell. Then she saw movement again. A creature. Some kind of wild cat, running toward where she lay, the slaver standing over them. Suddenly Nalissa smiled. "You forgot something," she said to Dracal as he looked past her and saw who was coming.

"What is that?" The slaver's jaw dropped in alarm. A giant cat, gray and sleek as velvet running gracefully toward them across the sand at a speed that defied logic. "Ralco!" Dracal's hand gripped his scimitar as he made to pull the weapon from its sheath but he was far too slow.

The cat fell upon him, snarling, tearing, scraping and ripping; the dying slaver's screams mixed with her feral savage growls. The Lynx had come to claim her fee.

Nalissa rolled to her knees, saw Ralco standing there, staring in horror at his master's shredded corpse. Ranysi broke free of his grip, and ran again. Ralco turned, started chasing after her but Nalissa grabbed the knife that had fallen from Dracal's belt and stabbed the giant in the right ankle.

Ralco made a gurgling noise and swiped a paw at her face knocking her off her feet. A few yards away the Lynx had dragged her victim into brush to paw and chew at the remains.

Ranysi returned, retrieved the knife and stabbed Ralco again, her blade catching him just below the groin. The giant turned and swiped with both fists, but Ranysi was quicker.

She hoisted Nalissa up with a strong hand and together the two women ran along the beach, the giant mute giving chase, best he could as the breakers surged closer, the tide coming in fast.

The beach narrowed to a point, rocks on the left crumbled into ocean, the sand swallowed by urgent water. The girls had nowhere to go. Far behind, Nalissa heard shouts and knew the pirates had returned. Father was dead or dying, and her own world came crashing down.

"Run!" Ranysi yelled in her ear and turned to face the giant, the small knife gripped in her hand. Nalissa stood frozen, horror-struck. "Go!" Ranysi shoved her. "No point both of us dying."

Nalissa nodded, and sobbing made for the rocks hemming the rising waters. She reached them, clambered up to a place where she could catch her breath. Once there she turned, saw Ranysi, the knife in her hand flashing, cutting through air—a shaft of sunlight trapping the blade. The swipe went wide and Ralco was upon her, his mallet sized fists battering the girl to the ground.

Nalissa saw Ralco strike Ranysi's body again and again until the sand was stained crimson around her. At last, satisfied with his work, Ralco turned toward Nalissa watching from her shallow safety. He pointed at her and made a chopping motion. Far off at the other end of the cove she glimpsed figures running, heard a clash of steel and shouts—perhaps it was those cutthroats fighting amongst themselves.

She turned, slipped on seaweed and mud, the giant striding toward her and leaping onto the rocks, a short heavy blade gripped in his hands, and a cold smile on his lips. He was gaining fast. Ahead was a wall of rock. She couldn't climb that. That left but one choice. The ocean. Nalissa turned to jump.

***

Silon was so obsessed with evading the men chasing him that he almost crashed headlong into the three wild figures running at him. And, too his amazement stared into the half-crazed eyes of Corin an Fol, that mile long blade swinging for his head, missing only by an inch.

"What the fuck...?" Corin blinked at him as the longsword whistled past and buried its point in the sand. The other men stood staring at Corin with quizzical glances.

"She's down there!" Silon shouted, and turned as a dozen Crenise emerged through the brush and raced toward them yelling. Silon allowed the three men to rush past him and followed on.

***

Corin had no time to register the merchant's face, let alone wonder how he'd got here. The pirates were upon them, and Corin felt that old rage rising up through his veins. Men like these had murdered his family.

He charged them headlong, Clouter swinging with pendulum precision. The first man leaped at him, Corin's swipe cut him lengthwise from shoulder to hip. He tugged the blade free, twisted, and stabbed through the next man's belly, ripping up and out until his guts spilled.

Corin jumped over the bodies and hewed left and right, severing a head from the next man, and stepping in close, reversing Clouter and ramming the pommel into the forth man's jaw, ripping it open.

Corin felt a savage joy as he slew. Time slowed. The world stopped spinning—no noises save the savage roaring inside his head. He had forgotten Nalissa, the merchant, his comrades at the station. Corin pictured his father's dead face, and laughed at the terror trapped inside his foemen's eyes.

He was dimly aware of people behind him staying well back. He lunged, swiped, hewed, stepped over another body, crashed into a third. Another scream, yet another dead man falling onto dusty ground.

Hack, lunge, swipe! *Kill.* Step forward, slice, tug blade free, and stab out. Corin snarled as he dug the blade two-handed into a screaming pirate's chest. He twisted, freed the steel.

Only three remained. These turned and fled back down the hill, Corin hard on their heels.

***

Captain Coralion yelled as he led his riders toward the Trading Station. He had taken only seconds to register something was wrong. The guards should have been present, but mercenaries were standing outside, watching them approach. Hard looking men like the ones he'd fought only yesterday. Perhaps the same men?

In his fury, Coralion forgot about his splinted leg and rode at pace toward those villains awaiting their attack.

"I want one left alive!" Coralion shouted as his riders crashed upon the foe. "Save one for questioning,"

He'd work on that villain himself. A hot knife, cutting here and there—go a long way to assuaging the returning agony in his leg.

***

These Crimson looked fresh from the city. Hagan could only curse Corin an Fol yet again as they careered their mounts into the station and commenced jabbing their lances, and hacking and lunging down at his men with scimitar and tulwar.

Quick-thinking Coly had found a crossbow and some bolts in a store house out back. He'd cranked and fired killing three riders before two others sought him out and their horses trampled his body. Coly screamed as he fell beneath those hoofs.

To Hagan's left, Borgil cut back and forth with the ax, his feet braced and a grim smear of righteousness on his face.

"I should have listened to you," Hagan muttered as he pulled a crimson cloaked soldier from his horse and slid his sword across the rider's throat. "And fucking killed Corin an Fol."

"Still time for that," Borgil jumped back from a spear lunge, ducked under and then stepped forward again, swinging out, cutting through the spear shaft and slicing the man's legs from under him. To their right, Dilan gasped as a scimitar ran him through. He sunk to his knees and Hagan lost sight of him.

Hagan saw Rejen fall, a lance skewering his body. Close by, Dol tossed his knife at a horseman catching him in the throat and dragging the rider from the saddle. He vaulted onto the horses back but fell as a lance ran him through from behind.

Hagan killed that rider but another emerged and urged his horse trample him. The rider's face was pale and Hagan glimpsed the splint along his leg. He jumped back, swung fast and hard catching that leg half way up and severing wood, bandage and tissue within. The rider screamed on agony and slipped from his mount. Hagan dispatched him with a backstroke across the throat.

He turned and then fell backwards as something struck him and threw him into a wall. He looked down, saw the spear sticking in his side.

The rider kicked his feet free of stirrups and vaulted form his horse. He leaped at Hagan, scimitar flashing in the sunlight.

Hagan tugged the spear from his side and the wall it was embedded in. He stabbed the broken end up into his attacker's eye and stepped past him to gut the next rider with the spear point, his sword lost in the dust and blood behind.

Hooves clattered, steel struck steel. Men yelled, cried out in pain. Hagan saw Strain the Rope's head rolling past. His killer swung a scimitar at Hagan, the sun's glare behind him. A silhouette.

Hagan shielded his eyes, cursed the pain in his side and ducked below the flashing blade. He found his dagger, stabbed up quickly catching the rider in the groin. The man pitched on top of Hagan and pinned him to the ground. His head thudded against a rock and he lost consciousness briefly.

When Hagan came to all was quiet. He struggled free of the dead rider and blinked in the sunlight. A shape loomed close. Borgil smelled as bad as ever.

"What's happened?" Hagan croaked, his head giddy and the pain in his side returning. He looked down saw blood oozing there. *Fuck you, Corin.*

"Dead," Borgil said.

"Who?"

"Everyone, barring them few riders as buggered off to get help. No doubt they'll be back shortly." He grinned. "Good scrap, hey."

"You're a sick bastard," Hagan told him as he staggered to his knees.

"So, what now?"

"We catch up with Corin an Fol and gut him open," Hagan snarled.

"You ain't going anywhere in that state," Borgil looked at Hagan's wound.

"I'll live long enough to kill that lanky piece of shit," Hagan said, but knew he was bleeding badly. He needed rest and water, and time to stitch up the hole. Only chance of survival, if infection hadn't taken root already.

Borgil must have read his mind. Kettle Helm reached down and heaved Hagan across his burly shoulders. The axman walked over to a stray horse and slung Hagan across its back. He clambered up behind and claimed the saddle.

"Thought you'd leave me to die," Hagan choked on blood and spat it out.

"Not while there's gold to claim and work still to do," Borgil said. "Your sword arm still works, don't it?"

"Yes," Hagan said. *And when I catch up with you again Corin an Fol, I'm going to cut out your liver and feed it to Borgil.* They left the camp and corpses of their friends and the Crimson Guard behind. Vultures were settling to feed. Hagan saw one alight on Rejen and pluck an eye from his head.

They rode until nightfall when Borgil risked a fire and treated Hagan's wound. The axman heated steel, scraped dirt from Hagan's side and cauterized the hole. That done he retrieved needle and thread from the soldier's saddle and stitched up the wound.

Hagan didn't make a sound. He focused on Corin's face and vowed the time was coming soon when the debt would be paid in full.

Chapter 20 | Aikashi

A rough hand grabbed her, pulling her back onto the wet shiny rock. Ralco grinned, raised his fist. Nalissa brought a knee up hard, catching his groin. The giant blinked. She struck out with a hand, raking his face with her dirty nails, just missing an eye.

He shoved her hard to the ground, his feet braced either side of her body. The sea crashed twenty feet below, spray whipping up and soaking her face. She crawled to the ledge but he kicked her and she screamed as pain shot through her.

Nalissa turned, spat up at her enemy, but Ralco smiled again, an ogre's leer; the blood streaming from his right cheek. He reached down slowly, retrieved a large round rock and raised it high to strike her, then stopped as a shadow loomed up from behind.

***

Strolgo was an excellent runner. In his youth he had raced down antelopes in the fertile plains of Southern Yamondo, grabbing their horns and pulling them to the ground, a knife ready—and fresh meat for his village that evening.

He lacked that speed now, but still shot ahead of the wild-eyed northerner and Morazzo, and the smaller man with the earring who had joined them. All three were behind, lost to sounds of crashing ocean, though Corin's shouts still reached him.

Strolgo ignored them as the brine washed his sandals and lapped around his ankles. The beach was shrinking to a thin wet line of sand; the sea reaching out and sucking at what remained.

Ahead was a man he recognized, looming over a motionless body, a rock gripped in one fist. Ralco the overseer. The monster Strolgo had promised to kill.

He shouted, the giant mute turned toward him as Strolgo—stolen scimitar in hand—vaulted up onto the ledge of rock, the sea lashing his legs. He slipped on weed, but corrected his balance and, angled his shoulders into a wedge, diving forward and catching Ralco in the midriff.

That dive would have tackled any other man, but Ralco grunted, stayed put and swiped down with the rock, smashing it into Strolgo's back and knocking him to his knees. Strolgo swung his blade, the steel biting into Ralco's boot just below the calf, and trapping there. Strolgo tugged at the blade but Ralco kicked him in the face and knocked him from the ledge.

The water bubbled around him as he tried to surface. But the sea's current was strong and Strolgo's battered body was washed out and lost to tide and shadows. If only he'd learned to swim as well as he could run.

***

Corin slowed to a trot as his rage slunk back down to a simmer. He saw the giant reaching over a woman's body. Horrified, he saw the rock, and then witnessed Strolgo's brave attack. He reached that ledge just as the brute kicked the Yamondon from the rock. Corin climbed, scrambled up the weed strewn sides, one hand gripping for purchase. The other held Clouter ready.

Ralco hadn't seen him, and was still staring at the crashing waves where Strolgo had disappeared.

"Corin!" He saw Nalissa's face for the first time, her expression a fusion of terror, hatred and joy. The giant turned, saw his approach, and raised the short sword.

Too slow. Corin leaped forward, slipped on the weed, caught his balance, slipped again but used Clouter to steady himself. He braced his feet, slowed his breath and then swung out wide, the blade slicing through air.

Ralco jumped back, laughing and believing himself out of reach, but the longsword's tip sliced his jugular open and the giant mute shuddered, slipped and stumbled to his knees.

Corin caught his balance again, swung a second time striking Ralco's head from his shoulders, and watching it bounce into the water, a spray of red accompanying it. The giant's body shook and toppled, a wash of blood mixing with the water.

Corin stowed the blade and gazed down at Nalissa. "You alright?"

"I am now," She glared up at him. "He killed Ranysi." Her eyes drifted over to movement behind Corin. "Father?"

Corin turned. Silon had clambered onto the rock, the Vendeli smuggler, Morazzo standing beside him. "My daughter," Silon smiled like a man spared the headman's ax. "You are unhurt?"

"We need to move," Corin said. The sea was rising, stealing chunks of the rock. They'd be trapped here in minutes, drowned or crushed between rock and white water. Corin looked back along the beach, which was scarce more than a skinny band of sand. He could see the Crenise returning to their ship as the tide washed over the jetty. *I'll see you soon.* A fight he promised he'd revisit another day. Looking beyond them, he spied another shape. A creature that resembled a giant cat loping off to the far end of the cove and disappearing in brush.

"Can we get up there?" Corin hinted the sheer rock face beside them.

"No choice but to try," Morazzo said. "We'll perish here."

Silon had helped raise his daughter to her feet. They stood huddled together, his arms around her and the girl weeping with joy.

"No time," Corin said to Silon who nodded. "You and the girl go first—if she falls, I'll catch her."

"What if I fall?" Silon flashed him a look.

"Too bad," Corin winked at him, and Silon looked for a hand hold on that rock. He pushed Nalissa up and then followed behind. It was a long slippery and perilous ascent, but they made the clifftop without mishap, though Corin, weighed down by Clouter, had slipped several times, looking down at the blue mass of churning water so far below and the white flash of seabirds swooping above.

He was the last to roll over the top and lie gasping like a beached leviathan, lungs rasping for air. "What now?" Corin sad eventually. It was Morazzo who answered him.

"Back to the desert," the Vendeli said. "The Crimson Guard will be everywhere—even if your friends held off those first riders." Corin paled; he'd forgotten about Hagan. *Too bad—can't go back there.* Morazzo was right. Their only choice was to venture into the wilderness and stay clear of patrols.

At nightfall they stopped exhaustion demanding rest, especially for Nalissa whose courage had finally left her as the horror of the last days caught up with her. Corin called a halt when they found a ridge covered in brush, allowing good views of the desert beyond, even in the clear black of starry night. He took watch on the ridge, left the girl weeping in her father's arms as they sat together, no words spoken. Far away Corin could make out the lights of Sedinadola winking like fireflies.

A soft tread behind. Corin turned, saw Morazzo standing there. "Sorry about your friend," Corin said. "A brave man."

"Yamondon." Morazzo spat in the dust. "An enemy—we've been at war for decades. But, yes, a friend he was too. I will miss him."

"Hard hike from here," Corin said. "Those Crimson bastards will be mad as ants spilling from a disturbed nest. "What happened to the slaver?"

"A cat killed him."

Corin and Morazzo turned in surprise. The voice had come from a woman standing several feet away, her face hidden by the night.

Corin reached for Clouter but the woman laughed. "Just dropping by," she said. "To remind you that we have unfinished business." Morazzo gasped beside him as the woman's body shimmered and morphed into liquid. She became a bird, lifting, great wings outstretched. An eagle, flying north and vanishing in the night.

"Give Nalissa my love—I enjoyed our time together," the voice drifted back to him out of the ether.

Corin turned, saw Morazzo staring in horror at the hole in the night where the bird ahead vanished. "The Lynx," Corin said. "This business isn't over yet."

"*Aikashi,*" Morazzo whispered, his face whitened by terror. "A shapeshifter from Shen. So the legends are true."

"What legends?"

"Far away in the east, a land I once visited as a sailor at the other side of the world. The men I met there spoke of creatures who'd once lived in their country. Shapeshifters and demons, their memory still haunting those living there."

"Demon or not, I'll gut her open next time she calls," Corin said. He was exhausted and hoped the Lynx would postpone her return for a few days.

"You cannot kill a shadow," Morazzo told him, fumbling at his waistband. Here, I brought you this."

"A sword?" Corin saw the metal gleaming in Morazzo's hand.

"A saex. A northern short sword to go with your long one. To surprise that demon. I took it from Ralco the giant after you killed him."

"I don't want that fucker's sword," Corin said.

"Wasn't his," Morazzo said. "He must have got it from those Crenise, and them from a raid. A northern blade and good weapon for close quarter work." He handed the saex over and Corin felt its balance.

"Well made," he said running a finger along the steel. The blade was two foot in length, sharpened on one side only, and curving at the tip. Corin stowed the saex in his belt. "Why not hang on to it yourself?"

"A gift to the man who saved my life," Morazzo managed a smile. "Keep it close, Longswordsman, and remember Morazzo the Vendeli."

"Thanks," Corin said. "I will." He slipped the blade free and tossed it into the air, catching the hilt deftly on return. "I'll call it Biter." Corin said, thinking of the Lynx again.

***

The sorcerer leant back in his chair. Outside rain beaded the windows and wind cried out in a shrill voice. He'd been scrying, using his fargaze to follow events in the south, a pastime of his while pretending to serve his monarch.

Caswallon smiled at the irony. Sorcerers were banned from the four kingdoms. They had been since King Kell sailed east over endless water fleeing the fall of Gol, over a thousand years ago. His descendant, Kelsalion III had no idea one now resided in his palace. Had taken up residence in the Astrologer's Nest, the lonely tower dominating the skyline of Kella City.

Kelsalion ruled the Four Kingdoms, but Caswallon controlled

him. Servant ruled master. Kelsalion was weak, a shadow of his ancestor. Diluted blood. A man brought low by loss of wife and child, with no heir to speak of except for a bastard boy Caswallon also controlled.

He'd done well, and had powerful new allies. But the sultan down in Permio was no longer one. *Too unreliable.* He'd withdrawn the troops the High King had sent to aid in the war, after the sultan sent word he no longer needed them. He'd also put paid to several spies down there assisting the southern ruler. Silon had escaped the net so far. And now Caswallon had more pressing matters to deal with. A vassal king had spoken harshly of him to Kelsalion, the words 'traitor' and 'murderer' branded in the air. An accusation that required prompt action on his part. Caswallon rubbed his hands in front of the fire. The man in question, King Nogel of Kelwyn was on borrowed time.

He looked up suddenly as a shape fluttered by his window, and the urgent sound of knocking struck the glass. A ghostly face in the rain. Caswallon shivered. He'd forgotten about the *Aikashi*.

***

She'd winged north through cloud and mist, the desert below meeting sea, and that ocean sparkling far below her as she glided high upon the thermals. An eagle, alone in the night sky. At one with her universe—which was what she did best, how she loved living.

She'd left those waters behind as rain and storm announced she reached the northlands in autumn. The city had loomed out of gloom, that lone tower a needle, the sorcerer's fire beacon beckoning her close.

She jumped down into the cold room as Caswallon opened the window. He looked distracted and pre-occupied, as though not wanting her there.

"How went your task?" He said, his dark eyes on the scroll at his table. She ignored the question and leaned into the fireplace, reaching out with a white hand, grabbing a glowing coal and squeezing till it crumbled in her fist. He watched her in silence.

"It isn't finished," she said. "The merchant and his daughter still live, though many others are dead."

"That's no longer important," Caswallon said. "Silon knows you can reach him anytime. If he's sensible, he'll creep back into one of his holes and stop meddling with the High King's affairs. Merchants should stay merchants and not intervene with the business of their betters."

"Do you want them dead—or captive?"

"Forget them," Caswallon waved a hand. "There's a king I need you to kill instead, a more pressing matter by far."

Ta-Kai turned on him her black eyes blazing. "You don't understand, man. I still have work down there! I never leave a job unfinished." She turned away, wrenched the window open again and jumped through the gap.

***

After three days traveling by night, living off carrion, insects and drinking whenever they found a water source, Corin was ready to chance the road. They'd skirted the towering *High Dunes* for miles before turning east and flanking the coastal cities until well clear of Syrannos.

Back on the road they entered a merchant's train. Silon carried enough coin to pay for silence and reports. He knew the other merchant vaguely, and informed Corin that word had reached Syrannos of the events in the Royal City and outside. Reports said those perpetrators had been apprehended and swiftly dispatched by the Crimson Guard, in a brilliantly executed maneuver. The sultan blamed everything on northern interference. Spies sent from the High King, who now openly supported Barakani and his rebels.

Apparently, the Crimson had thoroughly searched the surrounding desert and Syrannos but then returned, satisfied that their master was pleased with their good work.

The camel train reached Cappel Cormac ahead of any news. Silon bartered for passage on a trader for the three of them, Morazzo having left them at the city gates.

"Where will you go?" Corin asked the Vendeli. "Back home by ship? A long voyage, I imagine."

"Too long," Morazzo said. "And I'm used to these desert lands now. No longer a seafarer. I'm making for Agmandeur to join with Barakani's rebels, to help strike off the head of the snake."

"Good luck with that," Corin told him and they parted ways.

The trader left that evening. Corin watched from the aft deck as the stone walls of harbor and teeming city beyond slipped from view. He gazed westward, glimpsing the distant palms lining the rim of *The Silver Strand*. He was weary, ready for rest and for some recovery time in his favorite inn at Sarfe.

Nalissa joined him. Her face, though tired and drawn, was strikingly beautiful this evening. She looked older, wiser—no longer a girl. She reached out rested a hand on his arm.

"I haven't thanked you yet."

"No need—just doing my job." She reached across, placed a soft kiss on his scarred right brow. "Your father..."

"Sharing wine with the ship's skipper below," Nalissa smiled. "An old friend apparently." She kissed him again. Corin turned his head away, not quite ready to mix business with pleasure. A subtler softer danger, he'd been here before.

"Your father doesn't have any friends," Corin turned to watch the coastline fade as dusk stole the last view of Cappel Cormac's shrinking walls. "I shan't miss Permio," he said, shuffling over slightly as she leaned against him.

"Me neither."

"You did well," Corin told her. "Showed true mettle. I see why your father dotes on you."

"Spoils me, you mean," she smiled up at him. A sad smile. He kissed her—didn't mean to. Just happened.

"Well, I thought you were a tad spoilt when first we met in that garden."

"Didn't stop you having fun as I recall," Nalissa rested her head against his shoulder.

"You took advantage of me," Corin said, and she laughed out loud.

"You, Sir, are a rogue. But I do love you, Corin."

"Love?" *Love?*

"Just a little," she awarded him that impish grin he remembered from the night in Silon's garden. The day before he enlisted as the merchant's strong arm and courier. "Enough to want to see you from time to time." Her face turned serious. "I've been so scared, Corin. I never knew such cruelty existed."

"I learnt that as a boy," Corin said. "The day the raiders came from Crenna and butchered my family. This battered face and wounded heart are the direct result of that cold morning in distant Finnehalle. Leaving but a restless wreckage of a man."

"You're the best man I know," She kissed him lightly, a tear welling at the corner of her eye. "I think I need to sleep now." She left him standing there, watching the shoreline fade into darkness.

Gods I'm so tired.

Corin went below decks to the cot the captain had reserved for him. Lay there for a while then got up again. He found Silon sprawled in a chair, a wine glass in hand. The captain leaned close over table a chart in his fists. Both men looked up when Corin walked into the Captain's cabin.

"Galleys to stern," the captain said. Corin ignored him and sat on the chest by the porthole.

"I smelled the wine," Corin said. The captain was about to speak again but Silon raised his hand stopping him.

"He's earned a glass," Silon said. The captain nodded reluctantly and pushed the decanter toward the end of the table.

"A glass…?" Corin said, as he reached for the decanter, raised it to his lips and drained the entire jug. The two men stared at him with mixed expressions.

"Corin an Fol," Silon said, and the captain nodded slowly.

"The legend of the longsword," the captain said. "You are known in Cappel Cormac, and not overly popular, my friend." The scream from above had them rising to their feet and Corin making for the door.

He half fell up the ladder, the new sword—Biter in one fist. Clouter was resting idle by his cot below. Outside were sea and stars, the sounds of ropes creaking, decks moving underfoot.

Corin, looking down the length of the ship, glimpsed a shadow, then saw a man's body sprawled, his throat torn open and lifeblood staining the strakes. Corin leveled Biter, walked on up to where she stood, in woman's form, licking the blood from her fingers. She smiled when she saw him.

"Hello Corin," the Lynx said. "We've unfinished business."

"You'll not take Nalissa again," Corin said, approaching slowly, sword raised, wishing he had Clouter instead of this meat cleaver.

"That game is over," she said. "I have other affairs to attend, but came back for the challenge in your eye. You intrigue me, mortal. There's a wildness about you. A lack of fear—unusual for your timid kind." She licked her nails again and smiled revealing the freshly filed molars.

Corin lunged, but she leaped away and jumped over his head, raking his hair with those fingernails. He turned, saw her smiling again, this time perched on a stay.

The Lynx walked toward him but a shadow settled on the deck behind them and Corin heard a voice he knew.

"He is not your plaything, *Aikashi*," Vervandi said as she appeared beside him. "The gods have other plans for this man."

The Lynx's face narrowed, her features molding into a scowl of pure hatred. "You! Your kin betrayed my people. The gods abandoned us to such as these!"

"You turned to evil, Ta-Kai, serving the Shadowman. I tried to save you, Sister. But your cause is lost. And now it's left to me to tidy up your mess."

The Lynx snarled. "I'm not going back there!" She became a bird and tore up into the night sky. Vervandi followed as an owl, chasing the eagle far up into the blackness.

Corin heard cries in the dark, saw a single black feather settle on the deck. He turned, saw Vervandi standing there.

"I can fight my own battles," he told her.

"She would have killed you," Vervandi said. "Besides, I had my own score to settle with that one. Ta-Kai is safely back in the void." The tall willowy woman glided across to him and brushed his face with her fingers. As ever, Corin caught the subtle aroma of wood smoke, honey and spring flowers. She smiled.

"I cannot always be there for you, Corin an Fol. And your greatest task by far is still to come."

"I have no idea what you are talking about—or who you are, woman from my dreams."

"I'm your guardian for now," she replied. "My Mother will have need of your service soon."

"Your mother?"

"The Goddess Elanion." Vervandi was fading as she spoke, and Corin felt fuzzy-headed, weary and past ready for sleep. "But you'll forget this conversation ever happened," Vervandi said. "Such is the doom of mankind to ignore warnings and forget the past. Stay away from that merchant's girl—I might get jealous."

She laughed, and lifted—a white owl fading off into the horizon where dawn hinted pink lines through cloud. Corin returned to the bunk and slept until Silon woke him.

***

"It was an accident," Silon said. "The deckhand fell to his death and broke his neck. I saw the body."

"He was murdered," Corin said. "At least I think he was." The memory of last night was fading fast like mist over water.

"Murdered," Silon barked a laugh. "I think you need some leave from duty."

"And payment," Corin said.

"I'll drop that off at the *Crooked Knife*," Silon said. "Three days— I'll expect you at Vioyamis after that."

"For what?"

"You'll see."

***

Two months later a rider approached the gates at Kella City. Hagan showed the pass he'd been given to the guards and was waved through. Caswallon met him in the palace. A private study accessed via a back door.

"You are the renegade, Hagan Delmorier?"

"I am he, my Lord."

"Good," said Caswallon. "Do you tire of being an outlaw?"

"I do."

"I've a task for you then. Succeed and you'll not only get a reprieve but also land here in Kelthaine, as I doubt Duke Tomais would welcome you back. Interested?"

"I am, My Lord," Hagan said. "What's the task?"

"Arranging for King Nogel of Kelwyn to have an unfortunate accident," Caswallon said.

***

Corin sat back in the lounger, birds chirping by the fountains nearby. The gardeners were busy tilling as an autumnal breeze chilled the air. Silon walked up and surveyed his strong arm.

"You look like shit," the merchant said. "Spend the entire three days drinking?"

"It's what men like me do," Corin said.

"I've something to show you—a gift." Corin followed Silon to his stables where a huge stallion was resting his head on a half-door

"Fine looking beast," Corin said stroking the horse's ears.

"Aramateus."

"Odd name."

"It means 'hoofs of thunder' in archaic Raleenian."

"Thunderhoof," Corin smiled and the horse looked at him. "See—he prefers that name."

"Call him what you like," Silon said. "He's yours."

Corin was taken aback. "That's generous of you."

"Not me," Silon said. "I'd give you a donkey, but Nalissa insisted you'd need a decent horse when you return to Permio."

"I'm not going back to Permio," Corin said.

"You leave in the morning," Silon said. "In case you've forgotten there's a man called Krugan I need you to find."

***

Nalissa drifted through the rose garden, her red dress lifting in the breeze. She wore flowers in her hair and her feet were bare. She'd needed time alone. Space to reflect on what had happened. A soft sound behind her. She turned, saw the mercenary looming up.

"I came to thank you for the stallion," Corin said.

"It was the least I could do," she said. "I hear you're riding south again tomorrow?" He didn't respond, stood there looming. She spoke quietly. "Will I see you again soon?"

"I dare say—now and then. I do work for your father."

"Then we'll have to use discretion, won't we?"

Check out the series here jwwebbauthor.com and join the VIP Lounge for more Free books.

Enjoy this book?
You can make a big difference

Reviews are the most powerful tools in my arsenal when it comes to getting attention for my books. Much as I'd like to, I don't have the financial muscle of a New York publisher. I can't take out full page ads in the newspaper or put posters on the subway.

(Not yet, anyway).

But I do have something much more powerful and effective than that, and it's something that those publishers would kill to get their hands on

A committed and loyal bunch of readers.

Honest reviews of my books help bring them to the attention of other readers.

If you have enjoyed this book I would be grateful if you could spend just five minutes leaving a review, (it can be as short as you like) on the book's page.

Thank you very much.

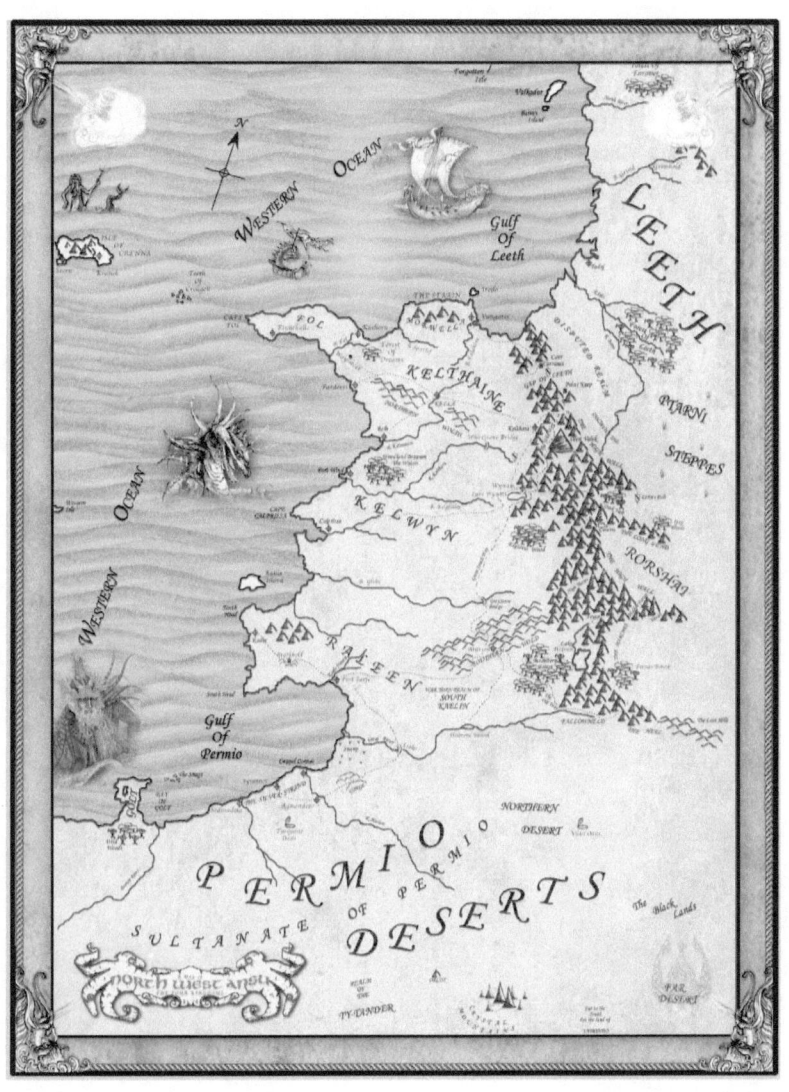